THE MUSIC DID IT

THE
MUSIC
DID IT

FRED FOX

FIRST EDITION ISBNs:
Paperback: 978-1-80541-662-3
eBook: 978-1-80541-661-6

Dedication

*To all the magnificent composers
and songwriters, new and old,
I wish I could mention you all.
You have more influence than any of us
can imagine in all ways, according
to individuals.*

Part One

James was a loner. He was about to turn fourteen. He had spent all of those fourteen years living on the farm and was still not comfortable with what, to him, seemed to be intense schooling he was receiving in the large secondary modern. He had, however, achieved a reasonable standard of education without much guidance.

Now was the time to decide what to aim for while he was still in a position to influence it. He was asking himself a lot of questions. "Although I like farm life, would that be enough for me? No!" he thought, "stuck in one part of the country! Office work of any type? No! That would be like a bigger school in a bigger town—boring!"

He did like music but could play nothing, so it would have to be a sort of management. Still no real decision made, he thought for now he'd continue with some carpentry. It would always be useful, and he had the tools and a few more years at school, giving him time to think.

Music was changing. It was the time of Bill Haley and the Comets, heralding the beginning of pop music as a very serious entity. It had caught the attention of all youngsters, including James. The entertainment value was there; while not entirely James's type of music, it was showing promise of being a money earner and business. Then, of course, he could always join one of the forces—again, very restricting.

James, no further forward, got up to walk slowly back into class. He took his seat in the middle of the room to prepare for whatever subject it was and accept the teaching quietly.

It happened to be religion, an interesting but largely misunderstood subject—not really something for James to get into, but who knows what the future would hold. The better the basic knowledge he had, the more useful it might prove. As usual, he listened and quietly learned as it crept closer to going-home time.

The bell went, the noise grew, everyone soon on their feet eagerly packing their school kit into satchels and cases. Transport, thought James, that's another possibility to consider. He watched the rooms empty, the buses filled, the bikes sped off. The bus James used took him halfway home, leaving another four miles to be walked through fields and woods. Tea would be ready and needing to be eaten quickly before he was expected outside again to perform his daily chores.

None of these did he question but happily did what was helpful. A lot of this was tough, heavy work; to James, the farm was a fitness and strength centre—two hours of training every evening after his four-mile run home. He was fast changing from a boy to a strong young man. At this stage there were not many things he would rather not face, including the town bullies. He was already finding them without looking. They, as bullies everywhere do, soon recognise young faces—a biggish boy with a friendly, innocent look was always a target, even if very strong, beatable by an older, meaner, experienced thug.

James had had a few brushes with the like and learned quickly to stay clear in any circumstance—for now, anyway. The next time, if absolutely necessary, James would be more than necessary. He would pick his time.

The weekend came with extreme hype, the film at the Rex cinema being *Rock Around the Clock*. It was Bill Haley; there had been nothing like it before. It attracted all the so-called teddy boys and girls in their regalia, looking for trouble and self-promotion. Trouble could be found or created quickly.

The film had barely started, with the first rendition of "Rock Around the Clock" completed, when at least half the audience were on their feet shouting along rather than singing along, stomping rather than dancing in the aisles, while a further number tore the seating apart uncontrollably, throwing the bits and sections everywhere. In no time at all, the whole cinema upstairs and down was wrecked. Why? The film and modern music must take the blame. This was to happen in every town in the United Kingdom, with the flimsy excuse of the music being the cause and therefore be restricted where possible.

Music again, thought James, has caused hysteria to a national extent. This music definitely had a dramatic effect on this particular type of susceptible mind! Another type of occasion for James to avoid, although it had no effect on himself. It was creating areas where anything could happen or become dangerous. There were, for James, better places to be with his preferred classical music and singing. Each to their own, he thought.

He soon met up with a few friends from his village. They walked together to the bus terminal for the journey home. There were still some lunatics around, high on the earlier music-fuelled antics, still looking for trouble. James and friends did not want to get drawn into anything and got safely on the bus. They chatted about the various things they had seen and experienced, both good and bad, now just happy to return home quietly.

James was up early for his work with the animals. It was Sunday but not a day of rest on the farm. The church bells had been rung in as tuneful a manner possible for the four bells.

On hearing them, James, for one reason or

another, always felt depressed. Churches in general, although great architecture, were depressing to him, and today the bells were no exception. He was feeling low—a form of depression by association.

James was an emotional young man, particularly with music. According to the music playing at any one time, he could find himself up on the balls of his feet feeling unbeatable, or sad and tearful, or a mixture of extreme pride as when singing the national anthem, also with very damp or wet eyes.

By the time his jobs were done, it was lunchtime. Ready on the table as usual. "One day," thought James, "you will have to provide everything for yourself in your own home, possibly in town somewhere." He tried to plan as much as possible for the next three years: first education, next a job to decide on, next motorbike licence, then a car. Transport being a must for any job and social life!

At the moment he was getting increasingly more fed up with buses everywhere and back or no life at all. Every passing weekend was making him more impatient for female company or a sex life. "I suppose one will lead to another. But hurry up," he thought.

Lunch was as good as ever, Mum providing

with a smile and never a complaint. "Your grand-dad is haymaking the ten-acre meadow today. It looks like a fine dry week ahead. Could you help him cut this afternoon? I saw him out walking in it; it seems to be dry enough to cut."

"Yes, Mum, I will wander over to him straight after lunch." He not only had a strong sense of duty but loved working with the old man. Within the hour he was striding across the fields to the tractor and his granddad, engine running ready to mow. He took his place on the mower seat.

"Okay, Granddad, let's go."

"Right, boy," and off they went. It took most of the afternoon but all was cut, ready to dry, turn a couple of times before collecting up into a rick.

That evening he sat having tea with his parents, listening to the radio, which was mainly music on a Sunday night, mainly nondescript for the masses with the occasional classical pieces thrown in. That night there were a couple of Beethoven's pieces, one of them *Moonlight Sonata*, the other the *1812 Overture*, both very much appreciated by James and parents. He loved them but would not tell his friends; it was not the done thing to show you liked, let alone preferred, classical music. He liked some pop music including the early stuff frowned on by his parents but was definitely understanding and preferring classical more than he would say to anyone.

They had a record player along with stacks of records and planned to buy a tape recorder player.

The early morning walk to the bus over the neighbouring fields often found him extra work. Today, being a country boy, he noticed a field away was a fat sheep laying on its back, unable to roll left or right. Experience told James if it stayed like that for long, sooner or later a crow or similar type of bird would peck the helpless sheep's eyes out to eat while it lay unable to protect itself. He scrambled over the hedge and field and righted it, still with its eyes. It ran off gratefully, without a thank you.

James looked at his watch; he was now a little late and would need to run the rest of the way to the bus and hope to arrive in time to catch it. As he climbed the last stile to the road, the bus was still there with its conductor, more than often the same one on this lonely route, watching for him.

"Come on, Jim boy, you are cutting it a bit fine again. We are about to leave."

"Thanks, I got a bit waylaid—a sheep laid helpless on its back."

"Oh yes, too much to resist, eh, Jim boy? Hahahaha!"

The conductor ignored James's protestations and carried on laughing. "Only joking, Jim."

James settled in his usual back seat for his half-hour journey. That back seat was always available in the evenings as well on the way home from town.

The bus was now moving slowly through the streets, nearing its destination. James spotted a music and record shop, a lot of signs and advertising in the windows showing lists of musicians and composers, operas and singers, with an invite inside to their booths: "Test and try before you buy."

James told himself in reply to this offer, "I certainly will straight after school."

The bell rang; it was 4 pm, his brain topped up with more facts to remember. He made his way to the music shop, the music section of his brain opening ready to receive different examples of music. The soundproof booths were mainly open. He selected some Beethoven, Mahler and Vivaldi to try two minutes of each. Headphones on, he settled down to listen. Suitably impressed with his choices, quite surprised at the different experience each gave, he came out, leaving the headphones for the next customer, and wandered round the shop until he found a compilation. The one he chose had the three composers he had just listened to plus three more. He was now eager to go home to the seclusion of his bedroom to listen to this special purchase. He was not disappointed!

Downstairs on the radio, pop was mainly played. Some of this he liked, but upstairs, and sometimes on the radio, he would have classical music, and this he liked much, much more, creating a deeper emotional feeling, the full range from calm passive to blood-boiling power rousing. His emotions were very controlled by music, more than he was to realise. In fact, an overpowering influence.

Over the next few years, whenever he could afford it from his various jobs, he would visit the music shop to listen to and buy mainly classical compilations, also favourite arias from all the best operas. Fast becoming one of his favourites was Luciano Pavarotti, who seemed to sing with all the best pop stars, all having completely differing styles and tones but working wonderfully together. Needless to say, the perfect tone and power of Pavarotti never failed to bring out anything less than total overwhelming emotion in James. The compilations he bought made it easier to compare and recognise the styles and different artists. James was always developing serious preferences and dislikes; he often bought any examples of the few main writers. His senses were heightened by chorals—male and female, and of course mixed. He was more and more impressed and sensitised by the power of vastly differing operatic strains.

Daytimes with friends he was enjoying and discussing the latest pop records and stars, while at home alone he was often overcome with the emotions provided by classical music, being sometimes reduced to tears in his lonely room, with his insides as satisfied as his brain was. He would have to call it brainwashing, as lots of pieces magically took over his brain and senses. After a session of his classical favourites, he needed to sleep it off, like sleeping off intoxication.

He had renewed and upgraded his music centre and would need to every few years as technology was advancing fast. His journey to school for the last year was made easier when finally he was old enough to ride a motorbike; he soon passed his test and was legal. Unfortunately, it would be another couple of years before he could drive a car on the road—that would be the warm, dry version of transport. Also, the cost would have to be met. So far, he had been offered part-time work after school in a pub bar. He was big enough and looked the part, and it would expose him to various ways of life he had not seen before.

He was about to come up against cheap machoism—the unintelligent bully trying to enhance their image in front of friends also of similar mentality. The more they got away with, the worse they got, like pack rats! For the first few weeks they were around, he managed to turn a blind eye and, more often than not, a deaf ear to their challenging taunts. Inevitably, the verbal confrontations were becoming too hard to ignore; it was all becoming too noisy. There was an ugly confrontation and the landlord threw them out.

The rest of the evening shift passed without problem. He said goodnight to the landlord and left. He looked round the car park for his bike; he was sure he had left it close to the door. He finally found it in the ditch by the road. He checked it over, hoping nothing was broken, and proceeded to drag it out of the ditch. He looked up from this vulnerable position only to see the group of yobs from earlier out for some sort of revenge. The jeering started.

"Well, well, there you are in the shitty ditch! Not so smug now, are you?"

James tried to talk to them, almost pleading with them to be reasonable, saying, "You had your fun throwing my bike in here; that's problem enough for me to get it out." He started to struggle, got it upright and was inching it up the bank when he was kicked in the back of the head. He, along with the bike, ended back where it started. Two of the yobs jumped in and proceeded to batter and kick him.

One said, "Look, poor old Jim has had an accident on his bike." They left him unconscious.

It was a couple of hours or so before he came round, the lights of the ambulance flashing. People talking! James was put in the back and taken to the hospital for the night, cleaned up, a few stitches. He rested until mid-morning, then released and on his way home. The landlord had collected him.

"We got your bike out of the ditch, tidied it up a bit; it seems okay. We rang your parents, so no worries. Shall we take you home or to your bike?"

"To my bike, please."

"How did it happen, Jim?"

"It didn't. It was those yobs from earlier; they had pushed it in the ditch, waited for me to try to get it out, then pounced."

"Let's go to the cop shop then; it needs reporting!"

"No, they will only deny it. Anything could happen. Get me to my bike, please."

"Well, okay, if you are sure."

"Yes, I am sure, and if it is okay with you, I will be in tonight to do my evening shift."

"Right, whatever you say, but although I do not think they would be stupid enough to try anything again tonight, we will see you safely home and no argument."

"Thanks, boss."

The bike was okay, and he rode home to questioning parents. He claimed tiredness but said he was okay and went to lie down. For once, music did not fit his current mood. He was depressed and felt a cross between helpless vulnerability and personal failure. Should he or could he have done better? He was sure some people would have turned possible defeat into a big victory. Instead, he felt a total failure.

The next week of school and work went without hitch. He was still plagued with what he thought had been a pathetic failure. At least he was back listening to his music; it was, as usual, therapeutic. Without realising, it was restoring his confidence. Now he was planning revenge. He would take his time; he knew a too-hurried revenge could make things worse. When he finally decided to act, no chances would be taken and he would not be caught! Also without realising, the more he listened to his music, the less mercy he would show. He was, without thinking about it, choosing the appropriate pieces. His emotions, with the help of Mahler, Mendelssohn and Vangelis, were reaching the perfect pitch—confidence to take on anything!

For the next few days he would be spending time carefully noting where the yobs lived and frequented. By the end of the week he would have chosen a place for revenge and hopefully settled on a method. Easiest and quickest, with escape route; he would not want to be seen anywhere near before, during or after. Alibi. Belt and braces, as his dad would say.

Time to go home, but what had he learned so far? Most of the yobs were drug users; also, most came to a dilapidated storage building on the west side of town to buy and possibly use. There were entries back and front, plus a small way out on one side. Therefore, choices with no dead ends. It was mainly used for large deals once a month. The yobs who visited it, he thought, must be working for someone else—a big wheel. There was no way, even between them, could they afford to finance the deal. This, he thought, was a professional gang.

His first thoughts were to create a bad situation between the yobs and dealers, leaving them to damage one another. That way no fingers could be pointed in his direction. Perhaps an identical bag swap. This was proving problematic, but he would take his time. Plenty of time!

He made his way home to his lonely but private room, switched on his music. He thought it would calm him down to clear his head, to think things through. First to play was "Va, pensiero (Chorus of the Hebrew Slaves)" from *Nabucco*, Tomaso Albinoni's *Adagio* and Chopin's *Nocturne*. By now he was feeling ten feet tall. Superman. His mind was now working in a different fashion altogether, the little voice inside was louder with its advice: "Why wait? You are big enough; take him by surprise. Wreck him with unexpected merciless violence!"

The music was reaching its crescendo. Time to go. He rode his motorbike back to town faster than usual. As luck would have it, of all people, his target was walking towards town. It was a great chance for an unfortunate accident. Without a second thought, filled with his inner feeling of hatred, he accelerated and rammed his foe. He crumpled under the collision. James was left standing astride the bike and victim. It could have not worked out better. Had he killed him? Perhaps not, but he was not moving. James began to panic, quickly looking round. His luck was in—no one to be seen. He made a decision: a few stamps on his victim would possibly be muddled in as part of an accident. He applied a few extra heavy kicks and stamps as he lifted his bike up, started it. Except for a bent mudguard, it seemed okay. He rode smartly off. No one had seen him, including the victim, should he live.

Home he went, put the bike in the shed to be fixed later. He needed his room and privacy urgently. He would feel safe there and divorced from any of the events. He chose the calming effects of Chopin. It worked. He sat comfortably, unconcerned. He laughed a little, but then the music, as it often did, began to fill him with emotions. He felt tears on his cheek. He questioned himself quietly, "How could music be that perfect!"

He played similar music for an hour or two until he fell asleep. He was up early the next day and fixed the damage to the motorbike. Had that really happened? Had it been a dream? Had he really done the damage to another human? Well, the marks on his bike backed it up. He would say nothing and act innocent. He had to go to work at the pub as usual.

He arrived, parked his bike and entered for work. The whole place was buzzing with the news of a serious accident nearby the day before—a man had been involved in a hit-and-run and left for dead in the road. Act natural, he told himself. Act astonished. There were several theories flowing around the pub but none in the slightest way pointing or suggesting anything in his direction, also nothing to implicate anyone so far—possibly car or motorcycle; nobody knew and, as far as James was concerned, no one ever would. Nevertheless, by the end of the shift he was glad to go home to relax in his bolt hole.

He sat quietly at first, trying to work out how it had all happened. He had spent so much time planning or trying to plan the perfect crime without chance of detection, and yet out of the blue his blood was up to such an extent he had ridden out—no plan, no care—committed a blatant violent act, then been ridiculously lucky to get away unseen. Never again. Must be more careful.

He would relax with Pavarotti, then sleep for an hour or more. He was not hungry, just sleep—that's all, sleep it off.

His parents had become more and more concerned about the amount of time he spent in his room, music blaring. He was going less and less to meet school friends; he seldom ate at home with his parents. He was becoming more and more of a loner. He did have real feelings for both parents; he tried to blend in with them and their ideas out of love as much as anything else, but the truth was he had nothing in common with them and, after half an hour or so in their company, neither had anything to say—just another awkward silence.

They were elderly and had had James when

they were old, which made the distance between them understandably greater. By the time he was driving, they were in their seventies. His mother became ill first and died. James took over the family car as his dad refused to drive any more. Without his wife he was not making a life for himself. James knew his dad would not last long; in fact, he felt for his dad and really wished his parents had somehow died together. His parents, very much like him, had been loners too. His dad, as expected, did not last long, and James was alone and in a position he had never thought about. As the only child, he was now the owner of a house and property plus a healthy bank account.

"What now?" he thought. He enjoyed his job at the pub; it kept him in contact with local news and got him out of the house. But really he needed a proper permanent job. He had always, like his dad, been a more than competent carpenter. That is okay, but he really wanted something to test his brain or at least challenge it.

At the moment his hours of contemplation were accompanied by passive music or arias that relaxed him without making him too emotional. He bought several newspapers most days to search for employment. But at the same time found himself reading the news, which most days seemed to contain numerous cases of injustice

with culprits often going unpunished or unde-
tected. He often found himself affected: "If no
one is going to do anything, perhaps I should,"
his avenging character was telling him.

He put the papers down as he changed the
music. He chose Delibes' "Flower Duet" from
Lakmé, *Swan Lake*, and "Vissi d'arte" from
Tosca—all beautiful passive pieces, just what he
could do with right now. By the time he was sat
in his comfortable chair, the music was already
having an effect, changing his emotions. It was
inducing a sad, unexplainable feeling deep inside; perhaps it was nostalgia. He loved the music
but it brought tears to his eyes—not a flood but
a continual dampness. Some music put him to
sleep; this certainly did not.

Two hours later he had prepared another selection of arias, mostly sopranos or choirs. These
were in the same mould and would similarly make
him tearful. Even when sung in a language he did
not understand, it was obviously the sound and
perfect tone. It would be a very late night before
he would be able to bring himself to turn it off.
He was very self-indulgent, with his heart saying,
"Just one more, just one more," over and over
again, ending with a mental wrench to switch off.
Then silence.

He was hoping to have a good night's sleep

but his mind still would not slow down. Instead he decided to go for a drive in the car left to him by his parents. He had fitted it with a radio with a facility to play tapes. Hence the saying: "He shall have music wherever he goes." And it did—sometimes too loud and annoying to people who wanted peace and quiet as they walked along the pavement. He invariably had his window open when he drove to town.

Occasionally people would shout, "Turn that thing off! That rubbish is hurting my ears! We do not want your fucking music!" Sometimes he would shout back, but careful not to take offence or become aggressive while using the car, knowing he would be traced. Of course, the day came when a man in temper threw an empty beer can through his open window. It hit him in the face. He lost control but drove on and parked the car. He walked smartly back to find the man. He was still walking with another can of beer in his hand. James had an iron wrench in his hand.

James met him with a smile, checked there was no one else around. The drunk looked shocked as he was struck hard on the head. His senses now lost, he fell to the ground, already bleeding badly. James bashed the man again on his unprotected head. The man was dead. James ran the wrench through his gloved hand and dropped it on the body. There would be no trace! He strode two blocks back, got in the car and drove slowly on once again with music playing.

He was thinking as he drove. There were problems with the way he was dealing with the drunks and bullies. He felt they needed to know why they were being punished and by whom. As it was, they knew nothing, and that was not enough!

He arrived home and was soon asleep. He slept soundly until nine a.m. the next day. An hour or so later he was riding his motorbike to his work at the pub. Once again it was buzzing with speculation of the latest murder on the outskirts of town the night before, and it was still the main topic of conversation when he finished his work for the day.

The local police station had been shaken again.

"This sort of thing does not happen here," the sergeant said.

"No, and now it's twice in a similar circumstance. Do you think they are linked?"

"I do not know; you are the detective—you will have to sort it out. I am a desk sergeant stuck to my desk."

The detective had already been to the murder sites and attended both autopsies. All he had was a smell of oil and petrol and a monkey wrench that could have belonged to anyone. He had questioned dozens of people and still had no clue. It had been six weeks and he was no further forward and certainly no link between the two cases.

"Two isolated cases, Chief," he replied to his senior. "Do any of their relations know of any problems either had?"

"No, no enemies, no money problems, and no wives. The first could have been an unfortunate accident. Now the second, definitely a cold-blooded murder. This can't be an experienced killer."

"Well, Chief, I think it's time to interview all the locals. I doubt this is anyone from far away. Let us try a twenty-five-mile zone from the town centre."

"Okay, just a casual talk to anyone and wait for clues. Both victims were a bit stroppy; perhaps they brought it on themselves and got more than they bargained for."

"Neither were said to have enemies."

James had recovered his composure and was back in the land of music, exploring as many composers as possible, discarding some as he got used to their individual scores, and at the same time making careful note of those who continually hit the spot, producing emotions to well up inside him. More than often, a solo minimal instrument would create what he needed, or a single male or female voice singing with intense feeling would also reduce him to tears, or at least an inner glow. His mind could also be overcome by a choir, as in Nabucco's "Va, pensiero." Today he would be interrupted by a knock on the door. He would have to answer it.

He opened the door; it was the police.

"Hello, I don't think we have met. I am Inspector Bob Thomas from your local police station here in town, investigating the two deaths, possibly murders, that have happened over the last two months near here. To be quite honest with you, we have little to go on and are visiting as many houses in the area to talk to as many people as possible, hoping to come up with a clue or two. Can I come in for a few minutes, mainly to hear what ideas you might have?"

"Certainly, but I doubt if I can help. Other than working at the pub part-time, I don't go out much. Come into the sitting room; it's more comfortable there, and I will switch the music off."

"No! Leave it on for a moment; it's beautiful! I seldom get a chance to hear any classical. What is it?"

"It's Mozart's *Adagio*. It's nearly finished, but please listen to the next piece; it's Chopin's

Nocturne in C. I hope you like it; if not, I will switch it off and listen to it later."

The inspector sat down happily to listen.

"Tea, Inspector?" James inquired.

"Yes, please, I could do with one. You are the first to offer today."

"Okay, kettle's boiling; won't be a minute." He was soon back with a tray. "Since my parents died, I live here alone. I still don't know what to do with myself. My music has been a saviour so far. Unfortunately, it mostly makes me emotional, but I rely on it more and more. Ideally, I would like to work within the music industry, but I am unable to play an instrument—big problem," he laughed.

"Well, Detective, you might not have solved what happened to these two men, but you have solved my predicament. I will choose an instrument and have lessons, hoping it will lead to a job, so thank you."

"Okay, James, I had better get on my rounds, but before I go I should ask: did you know anything of these two men or have any clues to offer?"

"No, not really, although I think the first one—he came into the bar where I work and was often a nuisance. He fell out with everyone. In fact, I think he was involved the night I was beaten outside the bar and left in the ditch. I reported it but no one was sure enough to name anyone. Anyway, it could have made matters worse, and I just want a quiet life."

"Well, that one was a known troublemaker who certainly had enemies. Thanks anyway. I had better get on with my job. Thanks for the tea and the music. If I get time, I will call at the music shop and buy some Chopin. I can well see it would be relaxing after a hard day's work. It certainly has a great effect on you, James, my friend. Bye, wish me luck."

"Good luck, Detective." The detective left confident that James was not a suspect—in fact, just a nice, quiet young man.

James spent the next two days designing and installing a quadraphonic sound system. Having done it, it was time to test with various types of music. First, the *1812 Overture*, then some pop, followed by Pavarotti. These should provide a good test; they were a success, and James was on his toes feeling a kind of aggressive intensity. This would make the next choices more difficult. Passive emotional it would be. It was appreciated just the same, ending with Debussy. James was back down to his preferred level, which was the calm content—a happy feeling to finish the day of trials. Chopin's *Enigma Variations* once again filled the room from all directions with luxurious music that would bring him to tears. It was now time to stop, get himself back down to earth in order to get some much-needed sleep.

In the morning he was searching with the aid of the internet for a job in the music industry. Also, he would search for music lessons; the piano would seem to be the obvious choice, particularly as he had been drawn to Satie and Chopin. He certainly had room for a piano and would have a chance to practise between lessons.

It proved to be a busy day. By evening he had arranged piano lessons, and a piano would be delivered within the week. Unfortunately, he had not found much in the way of work but it would be more possible when and if he learned to play the piano. No sooner had it arrived than he was tinkling with it, his mind was buzzing. "How on earth can I put these notes together to make music?" He was not going to be put off; as impossible as it seemed at the moment, he would succeed. His desire to play anything would keep him trying for a long, long time. In the first day he had managed a few chords and put them casually together. For this his fingers were being worked hard. He was encouraged and looking forward to his first lesson. He would visit the teacher's home, then afterwards go straight home to practise.

Saturday was always a shopping day for him: provisions first, then the music shop. This time he would buy some chorals to add to his collection and some lesser-known composers to enlarge his knowledge and search for gems to satisfy his inquisitive mind. This done, he walked back to his car laden with his purchases. Well satisfied with his day's work, he put his bags and boxes in the car, locked it, and entered the café. A snack and coffee now would save catering at home. He was halfway through his burger when joined by Inspector Thomas.

"Hi, James, can I join you? I am starving and need a break."

"Sure, join me."

"Thanks. What have you been up to today?"

"Well, my piano came today and I have booked piano lessons for Tuesday, and just bought some CDs—Beethoven, Mahler, and Mendelssohn—to test on my new sound system. If you have time tomorrow, call in—that is, if you are interested."

"I would like that but it would have to be early afternoon as I am working in the morning. How about I bring some beers and a pizza for us around 1:00?"

"Perfect, Bob, if that's okay with you?"

"You bet it is. See you at 1:00 then."

They both finished eating and left. James drove home to play his new music on his self-constructed quadraphonic sound system.

The music was good; he was seated in the centre to take full advantage. Two hours of this had put his emotions through several differing feelings, nothing too extreme but thoroughly enjoyed, with the occasional mind-tingling need to stand as though in applause. Today it had all deserved applause. Now he would carefully select the best bits to play for Bob—the type he knew Bob would like.

The next morning James practised the finger exercises he got from the booklet that came with the piano. He especially enjoyed the ones that required the piano. He was gradually believing he would become a proficient pianist. He practised until the doorbell rang. It was Bob with lunch.

"Come in, Bob. What would you like to listen to while we eat?"

"Something romantic today, James. I have a date and it will get me in the mood… I hope. She says she likes classical music, normally vocal."

"For us, Bob, I will put on some Morricone, then Saint-Saëns. After we eat, Puccini's "Vissi d'arte" from *Tosca*."

They must have been tired, and the beer did not help; they were half asleep when the music stopped.

"Loved it," Bob said. "Do you know how alike musically we are, James? Very! But for my date later I think I need something else to create the right mood."

"I'll tell you what, Bob. I will play Delibes' "Flower Duet" from *Lakmé* while I sort out music for your date. I like some pop a lot as well."

They sat comfortably listening while finishing the pizza. James got up and quickly chose some pop music with Bob's romantic evening in mind: Foreigner singing "I Want to Know What Love Is", then Roberta Flack with "Killing Me Softly", finished off with Pavarotti and Tracy Chapman singing "Baby, Can I Hold You Tonight", and for good measure he added Leonard Cohen with "Dance Me to the End of Love". They laughed a bit as they listened, finishing their beers, getting gradually more relaxed and thoughtful.

"Bob, are you likely to end up at your place tonight? Only I was thinking, choose some CDs, take them with you to play then. You yourself know how dramatically the right music can affect emotions."

"Great, James, I will do that. I am quite sure music excites her as much as me."

The music finished; Bob got up to go, chose the discs. "Thanks for this. As you have pointed out, music does create major emotion changes; we will see tonight!"

"Good luck, Bob. I am sure you do not need luck, though."

He left, work no longer on his mind, just looking forward to female company.

"I will enjoy tonight; I have not a care in the world other than pleasing Jenny."

"I am pleased for you and Jenny. I will probably see you in the week, Bob. I will be in town for my piano lessons."

"Best of luck to the teacher then, James—and you, of course, James. Now I will go and shower and change. Bye, thanks for the music."

"No, thank you, Bob, for lunch."

Bob left feeling good.

All this had set James thinking of himself. He had always been attracted to girls and was becoming more aware of living alone. Whereas most others had sought female company several years earlier, he was questioning himself: how had he been so preoccupied that he had ignored the other big desire in his life—that of female companionship? Now it had been brought into the picture by his friend Bob, who was excited at meeting his lady friend that night.

James thought, "I do have female friends to chat happily to. What's more, they always seemed pleased to see me. Besides the piano lessons, I should pay attention to the possibility of dates and an accepted closer relationship."

As he cleared up the house he was making plans to casually bump into his favourite girls while in town for his piano lessons. Yes, he thought, I should work at it now. He finished his housework and watched the news on TV while exercising his fingers for his lesson. He then showered and went early to bed for his important day out.

He was up as usual at first light. Living alone had given him this habit without knowing why. This particular morning the news on the TV brought misery or misfortune for others. Coffee was welcome and finger exercises practised. He attempted to play one of his basic tunes on the piano, thinking, "One day, one day." It was still early but he would make a move slowly to his lesson. He must have been spotted loitering outside the gate. The house door opened and a voice inquired:

"James, is that you?"

"Yes," he replied. "Sorry I am so early."

"No problem, come in. You are my first for the day and it will be nice to talk first, and background and what you want to achieve is important."

"Well, I am ready if you are." A happy James entered the welcoming front door.

"I am Joanna. What genre of music most interests you, James? I always like to know even though the first few lessons are always the same. After that, if you continue, it will become important to aim in the right direction, as an interested pupil is always the best and easiest to teach."

"Well, in a nutshell, I am very much a classical music enthusiast. Chopin I love, and Beethoven and the *Moonlight Sonata*, but I expect this to be months if not years down the line. But you did ask, and I am an absolute beginner."

"That's great, James. Most students, young and old, do not know what they want or what to aim for—from Scott Joplin to church organ. You, having spoken, James, I am willing to bet you have googled a lot and are already doing finger exercises, am I right?"

"You are."

"Well, continue with them all the time at home; they are good and useful. Also, can you use someone's piano to practise between lessons?"

"I have already bought one."

"I should have guessed," she gasped. "We are going to get on well." She beckoned him to a door. "This is the music room; come in."

The lesson started early and ran over time,

not that she seemed to mind at all. He had heard the other pupils arrive and said, "Should I go?"

"They can wait a bit, James. You, I think, are going to be a special student. Practise all we did today; go through it all at home as much as you can."

"I will, but one lesson a week does not seem enough. How about two? Would that be okay?"

"It certainly would. Normally people cannot afford to come twice, so I assumed you would prefer once as well. I will look in my diary then message you when. I think an early part of the day again, then you can arrive early again. Ha ha ha."

"Perfect, Joanna. I will rush off now; I have an urgent appointment with my piano." He walked apologetically past the waiting pupils. He hurried excitedly home.

It was only when he was sat at the piano reconstructing his lesson that he found himself thinking more of Joanna than the music. She was an attractive lady, a bit older than him but who cares? He did not! Also, now he thought she seemed to be single! But was she? Steady, he told himself, I must not get ahead of myself; the lessons must come first! Anything else later, if!

He sat in thought before returning to his practices. The phone rang.

"It's me, Joanna. Can we make it 10 a.m. every Monday and Thursday, James?"

"That's good for me. See you bright and early Thursday morning then."

"Yes, and James, bright but not too early."

"Yes, not too early!" He laughed and thought to himself, you, teacher, are going to have the most practised pupil ever. He returned to his piano ever more encouraged.

Part Two

Thursday soon came round and he was a bit early, although he had tried not to be. The same as the next few Thursdays and Mondays.

"Do you know, James, your lessons are going really well, but your main strengths are your understanding of music and judgment of timing and perfect pitch. Also, what is required of every piece we have played or listened to. I do not think you will ever be a concert pianist, but I do feel you do have a serious future in music somewhere. You are playing well; please don't give up. Music is already in you! I seldom talk to anyone, whether professional or not, and get the same perfect judgment and heartfelt response from anyone other than you. Don't get me wrong; I do think you will be a very good pianist. But there is much more in the way of musical understanding and appreciation. You could be anything you want to be—perhaps a choreographer or performance adviser, or choir master, perhaps my job—piano teacher. What, James, would you like most?"

"If I have a choice, I want to play well, but I would be happy with a job in music anywhere, a job as good as possible. There are so many genres of music that make me emotional—in fact, most music. Lately, I have found myself enjoying some pop singers and songs: Roberta Flack, Annie Lennox, Barry White. What about you, Joanna?"

"Yes, all of those and others. I play them all, but in serious times I get drawn back to classical and classical singers. For me, Pavarotti is in a class of his own and yet happy to duet with any and everyone."

"Joanna," he asked. He had plucked up courage. "Please say no if not appropriate, but if you have time one day or evening, I would really enjoy it if you came to my house where I will prepare half a dozen or so of what I call musical treats to play and discuss. I would love your opinion. I have a good sound system."

"James, I would enjoy that a lot. One problem with my job is I teach most days, and as I live alone it would have to be an evening from 6:00 on. You choose and I will be there."

"Okay, how about Saturday?"

"Perfect, I will be there. I am already looking forward to it a lot."

James left, thinking through his options, already in his mind selecting the music and the order in which to play them for the best effect. He was thinking a mix of Chopin and Beethoven, followed by more stirring modern music such as Vangelis's *Conquest of Paradise* and the articulate piano of Ludovico Einaudi. He reached home and immediately made notes, as more of his preferred pieces came to mind—instrumental and vocal—all he had found highly emotional for him. Sometime, he thought, he would have to whittle the lot down; it was getting too large for a week, let alone one night.

The one thing that he had not even thought about, let alone considered, was possibly the most important—that he would be entertaining an attractive lady in emotional circumstances for the first time in his life, definitely uncharted waters. Several different emotions at the same time. He must have realised how his emotions took him over in even ordinary situations. How would he react? How would he cope? One thing certain: he would find out on Saturday night, and so would she.

The week seemed to fly by. His meticulous character had ensured he was ready for his meeting well in time. He had played and listened to all the possibilities, gradually eliminating some, leaving his final selections in the order he would play them. He had bought wine and made snacks. Living alone had ensured he was a capable cook. He now sat quietly thinking, making sure he had not forgotten anything.

The evening duly arrived. He was stirred into action by the sound of the doorbell. He was quickly there, only stopping to switch the music centre on. Chopin's *Nocturne in C* was quietly playing by the time he opened the door. She stood smiling; she looked different—in fact, very attractive. She had obviously bothered.

"Wow, come in," he said. "You look good."

"Thank you," she replied.

Without thinking he kissed her on the cheek. This he had not done before. She seemed happy with the attention.

"Would you like a drink? Wine or coffee? What do you fancy?"

"Wine would be nice, thank you."

"Make yourself comfortable. I have our comfortable chairs in the centre of the room to take best advantage of my quadraphonic sound system. I will fetch the wine while Freddy Chopin entertains you."

He was very soon back with the wine.

"Thank you," she sipped the wine and sat back in her chair. "This is nice, and you have chosen the music perfectly."

"I have stayed with the piano for the next piece—Beethoven's *Piano Concerto*."

"Good for me, James," she smiled back.

He thought he detected a flutter of the eyelashes that pleased him. Beethoven finished.

"Now for something different. I hope you like Roberta Flack."

"Oh yes, I do—a lot."

"Killing Me Softly" seemed to hit the spot. James brought in the snacks; they were also well received.

"You thought of everything, James. Do you entertain often?"

"No, you are the first here. Now for my favourite—Pavarotti," he announced, "with Tracy Chapman."

"Oh yes, I love it. We are very alike, James—remarkably."

Next he played "Va, pensiero" from *Nabucco*, also received enthusiastically. They had not just listened to the music but had chatted and joked all the time.

"The music has changed you, James. You are now so relaxed. I am seeing a side of you I have not seen before."

"Is that a good thing?" he inquired.

"It is a great thing, James. Music creates all sorts of emotions in me, and I sense in you too. The musically enthused James is very attractive. I like him. It changes you, James."

By now Vangelis was playing.

"I don't want to upset you by being forward, but the music has emboldened me! I need to tell you how much emotional and attracted to you I feel. Please don't be cross; I am a gentleman."

"James, forget the gentleman bit. I have emotions welling up inside me for you. Perhaps it is partly the music, but basically, Jay, I am now very turned on. Do you want to kiss me? Well, please do it! Now I am feeling awkward!"

"Sorry," he said.

He got up and walked towards her as if in a trance and kissed her on the lips. She had both her arms round his neck, welcoming him. His emotions had reached fever pitch; he was struggling to control them. After some time he released her and stepped back.

"Sorry, I did not plan this."

"Nor did I, Jay, but I am so glad it happened. To say the least, I needed it. Now I am happy! I would like another glass of wine, some more music, and see where it leads. Okay?"

"Sure, Jo, you know best. What's more, you are in control of the situation. I am blown away. I will get the wine and attempt to pull myself together," he laughed.

Ludovico Einaudi was playing.

"Oh yes, Jay, your choices continue perfectly. I love all Ludovico's pieces a lot."

They drank their wine; it proved a welcome break from what was becoming an awkward situation for James. They discussed the music as previously planned. But less than an hour later and more music, they were back with strong emotional feelings, stronger than before. She now had joined him on his chair. He now wished he had put a settee in the room, but then her on his knee on his chair was excitingly personal and suited them both.

"Jay, if it suited you, I could stay the night, and would love to. And if it was left to you, I don't think you would ask! What would you like?"

"More than anything I would love you to stay. Please stay."

"I didn't come prepared; I have no night clothes."

"No need, I won't look," he joked.

He led her to the bedroom, removing his and her clothes as they went. She was a bit older and more worldly than him, and he knew he would struggle to control himself to perform the sex he would like to! And he was not wrong. As she lay there, welcoming on the bed, he started to struggle and barely got halfway into her before he started to come. It was ruining it for him. She came to the rescue with some timely encouraging words.

"Well, James, that was a real compliment you gave to me—a huge emotional compliment that I will treasure! Also, James, my man, you have a fine piece of manhood there. I will look forward to getting used to it all someday."

These words seemed to do the trick and he soon tried again, more successful this time. He did get right into her, long enough for her to have her orgasm.

"My God, Jay, that was perfect and I did manage to take you all! You more than satisfied me. All this and the wine, James—I will sleep well even naked," they laughed. Both were very happy.

They woke early next morning.

"What would you like for breakfast, Jo?"

"Coffee and anything. No hurry; it's Sunday and I have no work today and all the time in the world!"

"Stay there, I will arrange something and bring it to you."

"Breakfast in bed, Jay? How wonderful! I have never had that; I can't wait!"

He boiled the water for eggs, then changed the discs on the music centre: Jason Sitys' piano, Randy Crawford, Bach's *Sinfonia*, Chopin's *Joie de Vivre*, finishing off with his favourite Ludovico Einaudi. Music arranged for a couple of hours, eggs boiled and on the tray with bread and butter soldiers ready to be delivered with coffee to his still naked lady. She drank orange juice first; she was impressed. But James was more impressed with the sight of this beautiful lady sat still unashamed, still naked, loving her breakfast.

"Careful, James, I could put up with this forever," again she laughed.

They both ate and drank their coffee to the strains of the carefully chosen music that filtered through the open doors.

"Heaven," she said.

He was thinking the same without saying it.

"When we get up, James, we should try to play something together on your piano."

"If you will stay for lunch, I will cook soon."

"Yes please, that would be great if you don't mind. I will have to get home fairly soon after lunch though; I have a lot of housework to do."

"Okay, I should do the same."

Being alone for so long, he had become a good cook and enjoyed it. They ate well.

"There are not many men like you, James. You are what women dream of in every way!"

"Thank you, kind lady, but I am not so sure of that."

"Well, I am, so there," they kissed at the door, very happy. She left saying, "Call me, James. I will be waiting."

"Don't worry, I will," he meant it.

Midweek he rang her; they chatted for some time as though they had never been apart. He put the phone down and sat in a happy daze. The doorbell rang; he opened it to find Bob the detective there.

"How are you, James? I have been busy lately so had no chance to call. You are looking well—in fact, you look like the cat that got the cream. Any news?"

"Come in, Bob. I have my relaxing Einaudi playing. I have a little news: I have formed a bond with Joanna, my piano teacher."

"A bond, James? What is this bond business? Has she stayed the night? Truth now, I am a detective, remember?"

"Will you shine a torch in my eyes to gain the truth, Bob, and question again my answer? Probably!"

"Okay, now under duress, yes, I admit it. She stayed; we get on great. It was perfect."

"I am so pleased for you, James! As for me, I have been listening to famous arias as well as Chopin and Einaudi. I discovered some really great ones. I never thought I would, but now I think I am becoming the Detective Morse of this area. Thanks to you, you opened my mind to the power of music, particularly for relaxing and extending the brain. Music, as you said, is food for the brain. When I get home at night after a frustrating day at work, I appreciate music I understand and can relax to. I won't stay long; I have a busy day but just thought I would call you for a while, and now I am glad I did. Congratulations, great news. By the way, I hope she is the one—that would be really good. I had better get back to the station now but would like to spend an hour or two of music with you soon. I have bought a CD every week since we met and am enjoying them a lot, and like you, I am happy with nearly all genres. Bye for now, James," and he left.

James was thinking: I now have a best friend who calls on me and a lady friend who stays the night. All that, and yet six months ago I was a recluse. Life is so much better. I should concentrate on finding a job; life then could be complete.

He walked to the newsagent's and bought some magazines and newspapers to search the jobs vacant pages. He would search them all when he got home. As he left the shop he noticed two roughly dressed men. He thought he recognised them from the bar he used to work in. They followed him four or five steps behind, making sly rude remarks.

"Hey, it's little Jimmy the pot boy. He thinks he is better than us."

James turned the sound up on his headphones, trying to mask them with his music, but they were not to be ignored.

"Little snobby Jimmy, no friends... I wonder

why! We should teach him a lesson in manners."

He turned. "Now look, I never did or said anything to or about you. Why start trouble now? If you think I owe you a sorry or an apology, then sorry! Now I am going over the road, through the park, home."

He crossed the road. So did they. He started through the park; they followed, still taunting. The park was empty. He noticed they were carrying several beers each. He started to run; so did they, but they were hampered by the beer cans that slowed them down. He soon left them far behind. They gave up at a bench and sat exhausted to concentrate on their drunken afternoon.

James jogged the rest of the way home, very upset and disappointed with himself. He felt humiliated. He did as he always had at times like this: he sat, music on loud, listening, trying to come to terms with himself. As usual he failed, and the music—this time Vangelis—only made him worse. The emotion he now felt was like a drug, his temper welling up inside him to fever pitch. It was getting worse. He put on gloves, grabbed his short crowbar. He ran out straight to the park in an arc round behind the seat where the two drunks were still sitting, by now half befuddled with beer, empty cans strewn around them.

James looked all around—no one to be seen

anywhere! Without hesitation he ran up behind them, saying, "Hello, big-mouthed bastards, Jimmy's back."

They looked round. He smashed his bar on one head and then the other as they tried to struggle up, three more times each as hard as possible. They were dead.

Time to go. He ran in the opposite direction to his home. He threw the bar into a stream; he knew it would be found and lead the police in the other direction to his home. He then ran as if training round the park and back towards the house. Although he was aware he had committed murder again, he felt at ease. Mentally, his actions had been like an exorcism. By the time he reached home he was relaxed and ready for tea.

The music had stopped playing. He went straight to the refrigerator to find something for tea. He changed out of his jogging suit, put it in the washing machine. Now he was ready to eat and relax. He ate, then fell asleep in the chair— another trait of his. He would awake in the early hours of the morning, then go to bed to sleep like a baby, as though nothing had happened.

Breakfast late, accompanied by Beethoven's *Moonlight Sonata*, after which he began his job search: the magazines first, followed by the newspapers. He had ringed six possibilities; he would phone later. A lot had been achieved to find jobs. To get one would be the icing on the cake.

Straight after lunch he started to ring. It did not take long before he had arranged three interviews. None of the wages were very much, but some of the jobs were interesting and could possibly lead to something special in the future, and all of them were in the music industry or performing arts world.

This time, rather than walk, he chose to drive into town. For one reason, he did not want to walk through the park. Anyway, he had three different addresses to go to, and one was way out of town—in fact, in the next large town on the motorway, it was Bank. He had arranged to do that one last.

First stop, the music shop—a basic wage for selling records and CDs. It went well; he could have the job but should let them know within the day. The next was for an agent finding work for musicians and recording companies. There he was politely told he needed more experience and important contacts within the industry. The last chance was in the city of Bank at the theatre, as a labourer with carpentry skills, mainly for making and erecting scenery. This job he decided to take, as most of the time he could choose his own hours. They also promised him the chance of promotion to the office, where he would be responsible for chasing up and employing musical acts and groups to use the venue for their own events. On the promise of this promotion within a month if suitable, he arranged to start the following Monday.

As he drove home through the town, there seemed to be police everywhere. Bob was at the park gate. He waved to him with a quizzical look on his face; Bob waved back. He had obviously been at the bench where the dead men were found and spent the day looking for clues. James felt sure he had left none!

As soon as he was home and inside, he rang Joanna with the news of his new job.

"Joanna, I was hoping you could come over this Saturday. I will cook properly for you and celebrate. I have missed seeing you a lot this week—please come."

"I will be there, James my man. What time?"

"The earlier the better. I will be waiting—just come when you can."

"Okay, early to mid-afternoon. I am longing to see you. Are you okay? I want you as you were last week—you were perfect then. Can't wait. Any music, I don't care, and we might even get time to discuss it this time," she laughed. "Other things got in the way last time, but I am certainly not complaining. I need you, James—you make me feel good!"

"I need you too, Jo, in a dozen ways. The more I think of you, the more reasons I need you. Oh! By the way, Jo, can you bring some piano music? I would like to attempt a duet with you, to call our tune."

"Lovely idea, James. I must go now—my next lesson has arrived. See you Saturday."

He spent the rest of the day sorting out his tools, mainly for carpentry, to take to work with him Monday morning. The box was big but fitted into the boot of his car. It was important to be sure he had all he needed to do any job asked of him. This done, he cooked lunch, ate, and sat back listening to Jason Sitys' *Redemption* piano. It was very relaxing but interrupted by the doorbell. It was a tired-looking Bobby Thomas.

"Hi, Bob, are you okay? You look stressed."

"I am. My superiors expect me to solve every crime in the county in a week! Now we have a new one. Have you heard of the two men killed in the park while having a drink—well, probably a lot of drink? Anyway, they had their heads smashed by someone or some gang as they sat. Oh, sorry, James, I should not be talking about it or I will be in more trouble!"

"I had heard someone was found dead but

nothing more. Is that why I saw you by the park gate the other day?"

"Yes, but not a single clue or reason to be found. We have questioned everyone we can think of. Now I am looking for somewhere to relax out of the way for a while, and I thought of you. I always find it relaxing here, away from work—a coffee and chat."

"Come in, Bob. I will put the coffee on; I was about to have one. I was listening to Sitys and Einaudi! Sit down, I won't be a minute."

He was soon back with coffee and biscuits.

"I start work on Monday, Bob, and beginning to worry about losing freedom. Still, I will see how it goes. It is in the theatre at Bank, too far to come home for lunch, so I will try to make a go of it. They promise promotion to sales if I am reliable, etc. I won't stay long if I am just a scenery hand."

"Well, James, I am feeling better already knowing I am not the only one with problems. You will sort it out."

"And so will you, Bob. You will solve all three killings soon enough. There is sure to be a clue, a giveaway clue somewhere. I don't suppose they are connected in some way—someone with a vendetta, for instance?"

"No, all are very different. The first was a

road accident originally, then finished off to cover whose misfortune it had been."

"Yes, I see. But what happened to the last one?"

"The last two, you mean? Well, two well-known pissheads sat drinking—well, admittedly too much—might have been mouthy to someone. The long and short of it was they were battered around their heads so badly they were left dead!"

"I come through there sometimes but will not be sitting there after that, just in case. But Bob, will any of the dead be missed?"

"James, you have a point! They were all a similar type. That's a link. No, I do not think they will be missed, particularly by decent society. I will mention it to my superiors."

Coffee and biscuits appreciated and gone.

"I had better get back to searching the park to talk to anyone around. Bye for now. Oh, I forgot to ask, how are you and the music girl getting on?"

"Really good. I am cooking for her this weekend."

"That's good… cooking on gas too, I bet," he laughed and left.

James sat down to write a shopping list and menu for Saturday. Later he would drive to the supermarket, first making sure he was wearing nothing that he had worn in town before, as people's minds might only need a little jog that could put him near the crime scene at the wrong time. James was always meticulous in everything he did normally, unless emotions became too strong to control as in the past they had. Luckily there had been no one around; lucky because on neither occasion had he been able to check well enough—the red mist had descended and he acted without thought. He was certainly not intending any further act of violence. Yet he was aware of the dangerous chances he had taken. He must keep his emotions under control in any circumstances, including extreme. He still had not realised just how much of an effect some music had on him and how it altered his character like a drug—one minute calm, the next bouncing on his toes, mind racing like a world-beater, heartbeat drumming with music, needing confrontation at any cost, sometimes with tears in his eyes, passionate and stimulated by the music.

He was longing for Saturday. He was prepared—food made, music chosen, ready, clothes ready. Soon enough the time arrived and she was there on the doorstep anxiously pressing the bell. Almost immediately he opened the door; he had been waiting.

"Hello," he said in an obviously welcoming

tone. "Come in—you look lovely."

"Thank you, kind sir. You are looking good yourself."

"Coffee or wine first?"

"Coffee please, wine later. I am here a lot earlier today and looking forward to sitting relaxed with you, and coffee will hit the spot for that."

The *Moonlight Sonata* was playing gently in the background; the coffee machine was bubbling invitingly.

"Would you like to serve yourself, Jo? That way you will get the strength and mixture you prefer."

"Okay, I don't have a machine at home and will enjoy experiencing and experimenting with yours. I need to know, as I always intended to buy one but never know which; there are so many different out there."

"Please feel free. There are better ones than mine and better coffee to put in them, so suck it and see, as they say!"

She poured and tried and altered, then said, "A machine like this is good, and now I know what to look for I will search the shops. I am convinced I must have a coffee machine; I will use one a lot."

"I have chosen mainly piano music for today: Bach and Liszt, then Charles-Valentin, plus the old faithfuls Chopin and Tchaikovsky. Nothing too loud or vibrant, hoping it will help us with our duet practice. What do you think?"

"Perfect, Jay, but let us eat soon—I am starving."

"It's nearly ready; I will wait on you in ten minutes."

"Good, my coffee will be gone by then!"

He went to the kitchen; she could hear utensils and plates rattling.

"Do you need a hand, James?"

"No, all under control—nothing much to do."

He soon appeared at the door, plates in hand.

"Come to the table; starters are ready."

"Starters," she repeated. "Wow, I was not expecting a starter."

"Well, we have stuffed mushrooms. I hope you like them."

"I will, James."

"I do cook a lot for myself but seldom get the chance to cook for someone else, like you, Jo."

"Well, Jay, cook on, and by the way, I am very fond of you, and your cooking makes me fonder," she laughed.

They ate and shared a bottle of red wine, all to the strains of Ludovico Einaudi. Each time a new piece started he noticed the effect it had on Joanna as she remarked:

"My God! This does it for me—my emotions are affecting my nervous system. I am tingling all over; I love all these; my heart is racing."

James said nothing but was feeling exactly the same. They had barely finished eating before James got up, took her hand and led her to the bedroom. She followed more than willingly, removed her clothes, and stood there looking to him like a naked goddess. He was now also naked; seldom, he thought, could any couple have been so emotionally involved. This was love, this was sex, this was everything to both of them—nothing else in the world mattered.

He still could not control himself as much as he wanted; it mattered not. He stayed hard and eager over and over again, and she was lovingly demanding repeatedly the same. The music played on; he had put it on a loop. They lay there mentally exhausted, saying nothing—words were not needed. They lay there smiling lovingly at each other. They were both feeling more emotional than they said; to mention it might take something away from the moment. There would be other and probably better times to have love talk; for now their emotions were overflowing with the music without adding to it.

"I have made us a sweet; let me know when you are ready, Jo."

"No hurry, James; I am feasting on you, my sweet, and that is all I need for some time. I am happy—are you?"

"Very, Jo, very."

They both drifted off to sleep, content. The sweet could wait but would be very welcome when they woke up in a couple of hours.

When they finally woke and prepared to dress, they were both strangely embarrassed, covering themselves from one another.

"Why, Jo, why cover yourself? You were not shy earlier—you are still the ultra-sexy lady!"

"You are the same, Jay. Perhaps we were intoxicated by the music."

"Perhaps, but I feel the same now as then. Please be my personal brazen beauty again now."

"You too then, James. The only problem with that is we might get drawn back into bed. I could never have too much of you."

"The answer, Jo, I think," he said with a laugh, "let us dress quickly but openly and take a chance."

They both laughed.

"You get the sweet, James, and I will change the music. Nothing too heavy—have you any Barry White or Leonard Cohen, Roberta Flack, Annie Lennox?"

"Yes, they are all there. Look under 'Compilations' on the bottom shelf; you will find them and some all together."

"Found them."

"Okay, sweet in five minutes. We make a good team, don't we?"

"We sure do, James."

Joanna had brought with her a selection of duet piano music practice pieces, which she placed on the piano.

"Right, Jay, time to practise and see what suits us. I am very keen to learn a serious piece to play together as our piece."

"So am I, Jo. I love the idea—let us get started."

They tried several, then selected three that suited style and pace needed to be compatible. By the end of the evening they were playing one piece in particular passably well. It had been enjoyable; they had laughed a lot.

"Would you like a mug of cocoa? It's late and I just want to cuddle up to you and sleep, James."

"Ideal—cocoa and comfort. I will boil the milk."

They had their cocoa and soon lay comfortable, falling asleep.

They were awake early. It was Sunday morning—breakfast at leisure. The rest of the morning was spent cooking lunch together.

"You have thought of everything. You shopped well. I am never that well organised—this is a luxury. Sadly, I will have to leave late this afternoon. I must get back to my housework; I have neglected it and I have pupils early Monday morning and all day and all week! So it's my last chance to clean."

"Okay, but promise you will come for lunch next Saturday and the weekend. I have come to need you here with me, and not just to practise the piano," he ended a serious request with a joke, attempting to lighten the moment.

"Next Saturday as usual. I also look forward to it. One difference though—I will shop on the way here and then cook for you, okay?"

"Great, I will look forward to it."

He knew he would think of little else all week in eager anticipation.

James needed also to be up and away early in the morning for his new job. He was, as usual, well organised; he had loaded his car with all the possible tools he might need.

The morning was wild and wet. He thought it could have been a better day for his first at work. Nevertheless, he arrived there early and inquired in what order the repairs should be undertaken. There were plenty of them! He made good headway and even stayed late in order to finish some before going home. Nothing was said, and he left tired. The journey home did not take long but he was tired enough to go straight to bed; he envisaged another long day.

Even so, there seemed to be dozens of jobs lined up for him. Undaunted again and again he arrived early and started straight away. He would have appreciated a word of welcome or thanks for how he was handling things but nothing came. More and more broken scenery and equipment kept turning up with 'urgent' marked on it. And all dealt with, yet still no word of thanks or sign of assistance. At this rate there would be no chance of promotion or office work. He had started to mention the amount of work needed deserved at least two more maintenance men. By the end of the week he was worn out, his enthusiasm drained, work still piling up. His only bright spot was his radio with music most of the day. There had been little conversation; unfortunately, what there had been was complaints about his music. This was a theatre after all—unbelievable, he thought. It seemed to James he was the only person working for the actual theatre that liked music, even though music was the main component required to make money that paid their wages.

More often than not, if a fellow employee

or even a manager walked by him and his radio, they would without a word make it their business to switch the radio off. Gradually this was leading to confrontations, and a daily problem with regular argument! The response from James being, "You want me to repair all your broken crap as I do without any help. Then I need my music."

Needless to say, the different music playing at any one time determined the velocity of the argument, particularly from James. These confrontations coupled with taunts:

"You are just a labourer here—you have no say in anything. We do not want your music here."

"None of you are in hearing distance of it other than a minute as you pass through. What's your problem? Besides that, I don't always have it playing. Go talk to one of the bosses, not me!"

"We don't need to. We are telling you now: the music stays off because I say so. Silence starts tomorrow."

He marched off leaving James feeling insulted. He knew he was working well and doing more than he was paid for. This in mind, he made his way to the office to talk to any senior there. The manager was there and James explained the problems to him that he felt were unreasonable. He was met first with:

"What type of music?"

To which he answered, "Mainly classical." He also pointed out the unlikelihood of anyone near enough to hear.

He felt he was wasting his time; it all seemed to fall on deaf ears, the only response being, "Well, you sort it out with the others. It's nothing for us to deal with. Sort it out or switch it off."

He was shown the door and left in anger. He collected some of his tools and left for the night as usual.

He drove home brooding all the way. As he got close to home he saw Bob; he stopped the car and backed back to talk to him. He needed to talk to get it off his chest.

"Hi, Bob."

"How's work going, James?"

"Okay—well, no, actually I am pissed off. Ever since I started working at the theatre I have had problems. I am thinking of quitting. Nothing is good enough—they don't like my music, even though they can't hear it. The management won't say anything even though they admit I am completing more than expected. As well as all that, I think they lied—there is no chance whatsoever of promotion for me to management or sales, and that was the main reason I started working there."

The more he talked the more worked up he was getting. Bob intervened.

"Jesus, James, take it easy. They are being stupid but you will not change them—they are not very bright. Go in tomorrow, blend in with them. It's a job—use it for a while; it's not forever. Go home, have dinner and a night's sleep—you will feel better in the morning."

"Perhaps, Bob. Goodnight, see you later in the week."

He drove home, had coffee and a sandwich, and sat listening to the soothing tones of Saint-Saëns' piano and fell asleep. He was tired. Two hours later he woke, still in his chair but ready for bed. First he needed to hear Joanna's voice. He phoned.

"Hi, Jo."

"James, my love, you are late tonight. Did you have a hard day?"

"I just wanted to hear your voice before I sleep! How was your day?"

"Good. All pupils today were young and enthusiastic, so made it easy for me. What about you?"

He explained as he had to Bob. She came to the same conclusion as Bob had earlier.

"James, forget them—they are idiots. Go in the morning, ignore them, lower the music and come home tomorrow happier."

"For you, Jo, I will try. Goodnight, sweetheart, sweet dreams."

"You too, James. I will be thinking of you."

He was soon asleep, then up early but not all that bright. Breakfast as usual and an early drive to work, still not feeling any brighter. As soon as he was there he went straight to work on the latest repairs. He put on his radio but lower.

Within half an hour two other stage labourers arrived and made it their business to approach him, taunting him.

"James boy, we can still hear your shitty music. Do you not understand?"

The taunting stopped for a moment as the management arrived.

"Can't you do without music, James?" was all they said as they disappeared into the office areas.

Once they were out of hearing, the jeering started again, obviously wanting the problem to escalate into a chance for them to be violent. James's mind was working fast in several directions. He was not the boldest of men and had never had a serious fight and badly wanted to avoid one. He asked as politely as possible without obviously backing down.

"You do your work and I will do mine. We don't need to meet—we work at opposite ends of this site, way out of touch."

"Oh yes, you would like that, Jimmy, wouldn't you! You though will do as you are told. Switch it off or we will, and then we will switch you off too."

They were now standing right in front, face to face with James. Oh how he longed to be brave enough to punch one or both. His mind was stopping him, imagining all sorts of consequences. Okay, he had been aggressive before, but each time he had had some kind of weapon—first the motorbike and then the wrench. Also, this time there were two of them and they both seemed confident of dealing serious punishment to him. Perhaps they were experienced at this sort of thing and he, James, was definitely not.

One of them seized the opportunity and kicked the radio hard, breaking it, saying, "That has switched that off. Now for you, Jimmy."

The decision was made for James. It had started—no way out now. Without thinking, James rushed the one nearest, pushing him back. Catching him off balance, he fell to the floor. James knew that was nowhere near enough and leaped knees first down onto him, knocking the wind out of him. His fat ugly face with his stupid haircut now looked pathetic. What an opportunity! James clenched his fists as tight as possible, punched him hard as though expecting his fists to penetrate deep, again and again. There was blood from his face and broken nose everywhere, including on James's fists, wrists and shirt front. Too late now—he must make sure there was no chance he could get up or fight back. He was motionless—had James gone too far?

Now, where was the other one? James looked up; number two was standing as though riveted to the spot, eyes out on stalks. James got up, took one look and punched him as hard as he could, knocking him senseless to the floor. James felt proud; he knew he would be in serious trouble. But he also knew he would not hesitate to fight again.

"I am capable—oh yes, I feel complete."

People came running to the commotion, including the management. All seemed strangely polite and not willing to get too involved or take sides. They were all aware of the ongoing problems; in fact, others had joined in before but now all very reluctant. The manager alone spoke.

"Sorry, James, but I have had to call the police and an ambulance. We never thought the problem would end up like this."

"Neither did I. I had done my best to avoid it but they kept pushing and broke my radio and said they would break me. What was I to do? They attacked me—was I supposed to let them!"

The ambulance arrived first and took both away for stitches and check-ups. The police arrived shortly after to take statements—two in uniform and two in plain clothes. One of the plain-clothes police was Bob, his friend. He came over.

"James, what happened?"

"I tried, Bob. I ate humble pie for a while and turned the music down, but they kept pushing."

"Okay, James, I will see you first for your statement."

With that, he went to the manager's office, leaving James sat in the rear of the police car. The statements became more accusing now they were being made out of hearing of James. Before any of the statements, Bob had left two clear pages in his notebook, as later he knew he would insert statements he would say he took from James the night before—one saying that James had gone to him the night before saying that he had gone to the police station because he was worried that something like this was going to happen the next day. Bob was always prepared.

In the office, he was busy taking statements, all quite similar, blaming the radio even if they had not heard it personally. By the time Bob interviewed the manager, he was already annoyed and uptight at the continual accusations of his friend James. He finally lost his cool with the manager.

"Have you any idea of the talent you were restricting in maligning the quiet, intelligent James? Unfortunately, you have lost and will miss out on the talent he had to offer by not understanding him. He will never work for you again. He has an outstanding musical brain that would have been a real asset to your company."

"We were not to know that, were we! And now, for the safety of the rest of the staff, he will have to go!"

"Rubbish! You put him in this situation and did not look after him. Now, if I were you or them, I would think hard before trying to bring any charges against him, as I see this as a frightened self-defence. Last night he came to us at the station and made a statement that he was frightened after what had happened yesterday—that he would be attacked, and now it has happened. He had asked the manager here for help but you ignored him. Perhaps he went too far, but we see that as an act of a man very inexperienced. He did not know what he was doing or how far he needed to go to protect himself. It is a very big indictment on you, sir—you did not stop to help or understand him and what was going on or what he was going through. You let him down. We will take him into the station for questioning but hope we hear nothing more about it. Goodnight."

He left. Outside, he spoke to the sergeant.

"Take him to the station. I will collect his tools and follow you with his car, okay?"

"James, give me your keys. I will see you at my office in half an hour."

Both cars finally left. At the station, Bob cleverly filled in the blank pages in his notebook in the form of a worried James predicting a possible attack on him. Then, on a fresh page, he proceeded to take the statement that James was now making. Whatever James was saying made very little difference to what Bob was writing; he was making sure the two statements backed one another up properly. All was finished in the hour. James was free to go.

"See you later in the week, James. Don't worry—all should be well, pal. I know you well enough; there was no intended malice or hurt from you."

"Thanks, Bob. Sorry for all the trouble. Tomorrow I will start my search for another job, but right now, how do I explain to Joanna? I feel I have let her down badly."

He drove home to face the music. When he arrived, he phoned Joanna. He felt she understood; her final words were:

"It's okay, James. We will talk when I come over on Saturday. I am more eager to see you now than ever. Get some rest. Love you. Do not rush into anything for a while—you deserve better than working for that theatre."

He put down the phone and went to sleep listening to Beethoven's *Fifth Symphony, Pathétique*. It seemed to relax him. He slept well and was completely back to normal in the morning. He was relieved not to be rushing to work as he had been doing lately. He lounged around most of the morning. He would go to the paper shop in the afternoon to once again check the jobs vacant columns in the papers, but before that, lunch with visitor Bob, who was still pressing for the fight the day before to be forgotten without prosecution.

But Bob had the lingering worry in the back of his mind about the ferocity James had dealt and the considerable damage to the two faces he had done. Knowing James as he did, he found it hard to believe.

"I believe you were driven to it, James, but did you mean to do the damage you did? Have you done it before?"

"There were two of them. I was frightened to stop in case I got killed. I have never had a fight before, even at school—other than the occasional wrestle but never a fistfight."

"After we finish lunch, I am going to the

theatre again to check things over and make sure they are not pressing charges. Is there anything you want me to pick up from them while I am there?"

"No thanks. I have all my tools and they can keep whatever paltry wages they owe me. I just want to move on and forget them. I am off to town to get papers to look for another job. I don't hold out much hope of finding anything decent."

"Your carpentry is good, James. Why not offer your services here? You have the workshops and machinery and only yourself to hear your music."

"I had thought of that, Bob, and also if I have some tanks with caustic in, I could do dip strip of doors and furniture. I have a winch in there to make any lifting in easy. I will make a heavy metal frame to put things in and help to sink them as well. I will still go to town to get papers, but thinking about it, I fancy working here."

"Okay, James, I will love you and leave you. We had better both get on now. I will call tomorrow sometime to let you know how I got on at the theatre."

They both left—Bob to work and James to town for the papers, even though he knew there would be nothing available. With this in mind, James changed direction to the local ironmonger's where he bought a large metal tank and ordered an angle iron frame, all to be delivered by the weekend. Only then did he go for the papers and job search. He had already decided to build a dip strip facility in the barn. Okay, if a job turned up then he would take it, but meanwhile to build a business at home and hope it would develop. As it happened, there was nothing for him in the papers, so perhaps he had made the right decision.

The end of the week arrived along with the tank and frame. An hour later it was in place with a winch above connected to the frame. The farmers' supply shop were about to deliver a dozen bags of caustic pearls. He would add some to the one thousand gallons of water he had already put into the tank. He would finish it all off after the weekend. Right now he was to have a visit from Bob, then a few hours to prepare for his usual visit from his beloved Joanna.

Bob arrived and put his mind at rest—the problem at his last job had been handled and would be forgotten, so he was off the hook for that.

Bob was impressed with the new set-up that James had built. He congratulated him.

"Looks good, James. I am sure it will be a success, and here you will not have any complaints if you decide to have music while you work or not."

"It should be up and running by Monday night, so all being well, Tuesday I will advertise the facility in the local paper and billboards around town. Then I will sit back to await the rush."

"I will leave you to it then, James. Good luck with the weekend—love to Joanna. I will get back to the office now to sign myself off for the week. I hope it's a quiet one for me this time, no nasty surprises."

"See you in the week then, Bob."

With that, James cleaned himself up and went to the supermarket for the provisions he would need for him and Joanna. On coming back, he watched the news before playing some CDs until bedtime. He slept well as usual and woke happy. Other than some cooking, he planned a lazy morning, just anxious to see Joanna. With Rachmaninoff's *Piano Concerto* playing in the background to casually prepare him for what was going to be a really longed-for meeting with his lady that he was finding difficult to do without all week. Just weekends was now not enough; he loved his music but needed Joanna as much if not more. Perhaps he should tell her how much he felt for her… well, yes, he would!

She arrived right on time. He was so happy to

see her but he still had not plucked up the courage to tell her how he felt. However, his cooking
had improved a lot and they ate well. Now they
were sat cuddled up, half asleep on the settee
listening to Barry White. James was feeling very
affected by this CD—something was welling up
inside him, not just confidence but full of emotion as well. He looked at her and saw in her eyes
she was feeling the same. She looked lovingly at
him but said nothing. His emotion had reached
the pitch that loosened his tongue and given him
unstoppable courage.

"I love you, Jo… more every time I see you."

"Me too, James. I might not have said anything but I feel just the same."

"It's not just the Barry White effect, Jo," he
laughed.

"No, it's more real than that, James, but I dare
say Barry has made it impossible to ignore."

"Yes, big bad Barry," they both laughed.

This was another music-enthused happy
weekend, both feeling ever closer to one another.
Even so, James was looking forward to starting
his new project.

Monday morning he started early, mixing the
caustic pearls and adding them to the water in the
tank. He had placed a large gas ring underneath to
heat the mixture when and if necessary. He need

not have bothered; the pearls when mixed with water heated the mixture more than enough for a month or so. He was learning that in most cases a cool mixture works well enough. A hot mixture could need watching in case it was too effective, and of course a large gas ring like that was expensive to have on much.

The next job would be to find some test cases, which meant taking some inside doors off. He sank a few things in the mixture; he would leave them to soak for a maximum of twelve hours then pressure wash them off. These test cases were soon stripped and washed clean in and out. Next, they had to be dried slowly. Too fast and they could warp. He leaned them upright inside the barn with the barn doors open—plenty of air circulation. Within a few hours they were drying enough to claim a success. He was ready for business, so he drove to town.

First, the newspaper office to place an ad for a month. Then he visited shops with billboards to place copies of his dip stripping services available along with his phone number. On the way home he collected some cans of wax in case some customers wanted their doors waxed—best to be prepared, he thought.

The very next day he started getting phone calls, some serious, some just nosy. By the end of the week, thanks to the newspaper, he started to get deliveries with requests for his services. It was not long before he was getting a steady flow of business.

"This is better than going to work every day and I am my own boss. I like this job, and I have music while I work when I want without complaint."

Bob called regularly and was pleased to see his pal James settled, earning a good living, back to his old happy self.

"Hey, Bob, any success on the murder cases?"

"No, still looking but nothing. So we are getting more involved in the usual petty crimes and robberies. I have a feeling we will never learn what really happened. The only clue we have so far is that they were all similar cheap troublemakers. My boss has started to think that someone is on a mission to remove all rubbish characters from the area. Whereas me, I think that is too convenient. I think troublemakers they were but just picked on the wrong person and lost out badly. Anyway, enough of all that. How about you and Joanna—still all good?"

"Oh yes, and keeps getting better. I am still practising the piano and every weekend we play duets together. I can see us getting hitched in the future. I have a feeling she is almost as eager as me. Tomorrow is Saturday and she will be arriving for the weekend as usual! How are you and your lady, Bob—still okay?"

"Yes, the same one, all good. We have settled into a routine; it's like being an old married couple. We seem to like all the same things."

"How about music, Bob—any classical or just pop?"

"Some classical but not as much as me."

"I was thinking, Bob, how about you two coming to us for lunch Saturday or Sunday? We would like it and I could sort out the music I think she would like. What do you think?"

"A great idea, but I will check with her first. Even so, it would have to be Sunday; tomorrow is a bit too soon. I will let you know tomorrow if it's okay."

"Sure, Bob, do your best."

"I will; I am almost certain she will say yes."

"And Bob, when you get a chance, listen to Gustav Mahler's *Fifth* or Rachmaninoff's *Second Piano Concerto*. They are both a bit too heavy for your good lady but I think you will like them. I will try one of our nuance pianists when you bring her, and mainly pop I think we all like. And perhaps a classical voice to test."

"Sounds good to me, James. I will call you tomorrow. I will be off now back to work in time to clock off," he laughed.

James loaded the tanks again with doors and bits to strip overnight, and went indoors to clean up for the day, to relax with music from Morricone. He would have an early night as he would be up early in the morning to wash off the stripped pieces, to put them in position to dry all in time to wash up and prepare for Joanna's visit. Lunch needed to be in or near the oven by half past eleven at the latest, and she seemed to arrive earlier each weekend. He was certainly not complaining about that, but he always needed to be prepared.

At first light he was up and working. An hour later he was back inside, washed up with clean clothes on but still too early to start cooking. He relaxed in his chair; unfortunately, the early rising and work was enough—he fell asleep only to be awakened by the doorbell, announcing the arrival of Joanna.

"Sorry, Jo, I was asleep. I worked early and sat waiting for you, my love."

"Are you okay now, James, or do you need to rest?"

"No, I am not tired—just lazy and comfortable. How are you?"

"Pretty good, apart from my neighbours—they are still a problem. This time it's my customers parking in the road, then they have difficulty parking. But the latest problem is they claim the music practices are too loud and annoying."

"That's ridiculous, Jo—you are not teaching drums or any loud instrument, and you have been there teaching for years, long before they arrived."

"Let's forget them for now, James—it's our time today."

"I will pop the dinner in the oven; it will take a while then we can eat. By the way, Jo, I hope it's all right with you but I asked Bob and his lady for Sunday lunch tomorrow and he rang earlier to check that it was still okay."

"Lovely, James—we can be an entertaining couple now. I am looking forward to it."

"That's a relief, as I am too."

Saturday went with the usual treats and pleasantries; they were closer than ever. Bedtime and no sex was a landmark, but the love was even better—finally sleeping, him first, with her looking lovingly up into his eyes before succumbing to the comfort easing her to sleep.

He woke as usual before six a.m. with a world of worries; this always happened the same every day. Usually he would have been laid awake worrying more than often unnecessarily, but his mind at that time of day would always find something to worry about. Now amongst other things was a new nag—this was the troublesome neighbour Joanna had.

What should he do about it? Should he fix it? Firstly, he would not want them to know it was him, as that would only make it worse for her. Before she woke he had made up his mind to watch and follow the neighbour and find a place or situation to punish him.

"Good morning, sweetheart," Jo said; she was now awake.

"Let us slumber here for a while, Jo, I am not ready to let you go yet."

"Suits me, James."

"Jo, which neighbour are the problem—the ones on the left or the right of you?"

"The left, James. The others I never see; they look happy enough and are always polite."

They were soon up, music in the background that she had chosen. He cooked breakfast while she made coffee.

"This is the life, Jo."

"It certainly is, James."

They sat around for a while and still had time to practise their duet. Lunch was nearly cooked when Bob arrived with his lady friend.

"Good morning, you two. This is Diana… meet James and Joanna."

"Hi… it's good to meet you both. Bob has told me lots about you."

"I hope you are hungry, Diana—lunch is nearly ready."

"Oh yes, we are ready, aren't we, Bob?"

"Go through to the dining room; the table is laid ready. We will bring the plates through! What would you like to drink? We have red and white wine and plenty of water."

"We would like water with lunch then perhaps wine after."

"That's the same as us. Help yourselves; food is on the way."

Lunch finished, they returned to the sitting/ music room as James called it. They all four sat happily together with their wine.

"Bob, have you had any complaints about parking or loud music from Joanna's neighbour?"

"Well, I was not going to mention it but we have. Luckily I was on duty at the time and was able to explain Joanna had permission to run her business there and also piano music was well below the acceptable decibel limit. They seemed a miserable couple anyway. I sent them on their way, but you never know what people like that are prepared to do in future. Why did you ask?"

"Well, they have been complaining to Joanna and have been quite unpleasant, so we just wondered."

"Well, they are in the wrong but we can do very little to stop them being unpleasant. We will keep an eye out though."

"Thanks, Bob. But now we would like to test your patience by playing a section of our duet we have been practising. I hope you don't mind— you are our first audience," they all laughed.

"Please play—we would love to listen. We did not expect entertainment, did we, Di?"

"No, but please carry on—I really like the idea."

James and Joanna sat at the piano and laughed and joked a bit. When they began to play they both became very serious. They played well.

Thursday lunchtime he arrived at her house, hoping she would be able to have a break with time to talk and plan a much-needed getaway.

"Well, Jo, I will pick you up Friday evening at 6 p.m. I have an idea where to go first. We will need an overnight bag, then drive back Sunday night."

"You are being secretive, James, but I will be ready."

"No, I am not being secretive but just happy to go away for the weekend for a change."

He went back to work knowing he would have plenty to arrange and also a busy day Friday before the shower and change of clothes in time to collect Joanna. As usual, he managed and still found himself early in the car waiting close to her house. James was always early; today was no exception. She was early as well this time, in anticipation. They had allowed enough time and arrived at the hotel early.

"Are we going near to here, James? What is this treat? I spotted your picnic baskets in the back and we are in the outskirts of London. I cannot imagine but am happy to leave it to you, James—anything will be good!"

The next day they stayed at the hotel and had lunch. Soon after that, they were off to the park early as advised. Happily, they parked in the large car park and walked to the office to collect their tickets. Carrying their baskets and blanket, they followed the arrows to the centre of the park. They made note of the toilets on the way for future reference, then over a walkway bridge possibly thirty feet high.

"Wow, I would not want to fall from here, James."

"No, it is quite high."

Fifty metres after the bridge and they were in the park itself. They picked their spot to spread the blanket.

"It's a good job we got here soon, Jo. There

are a lot of people here already and most of the best spots are taken."

"Whatever it is, it is very popular."

"It's a concert. If you look down at the lake, there is a large stage stretching out over the water with all the seats for the musicians. They will arrive in a couple of hours to entertain us late afternoon and evening. Along with the tickets, I picked up a brochure for the event for us to read. You go first; I will be mother. What would you like to drink? Hot or cold—I brought both."

"Coffee now, James, then cold with the picnic. I am not hungry yet; our meal at the hotel was filling. Another hour and I will be feeling peckish."

"This is lovely, James. With the sun on the lake, I can't wait for the music. I see that they are going to play the piano concertos of both composers and string sections, plus a few unknown pieces—unknown to me, that is."

Time passed quite quickly. Soon the musicians moved in and were tuning and warming up their various instruments before a conductor arrived to applause. The couple stopped eating to listen. A few introductory words, then soon enough the music was in full flow. It was magical; they were both enthralled. Unfortunately, not everyone had come for the music, and some of the noise and antics made it hard to hear the music. The group of people sat behind, although possibly ten metres away, were affecting all the others around them. After putting up with this for an hour, James, in the middle of an intermission, turned round to them and politely asked them to quieten a little for the sake of others. This was met with abuse and:

"Do you own the park?"

"Just having to look at the rear of you two puts us off, so mind your own business—don't tell us what to do."

"Leave it, James. They are ignorant and probably drunk. Let us enjoy what we can—ignore them," James smiled back at her but inside he was knotted up.

The music started up again, but a cork from a bottle was thrown towards them, then another. This seemed to amuse them, so they threw more bits. James chose to act unaware and absorbed in the music, but he had been watching them out of the corner of his eye. The alcohol that group had been absorbing was about to play its part. The loudest of the group got up to stagger to the toilet.

"Jo, I won't be a minute—I need to go to the toilet. Will you be okay?"

"Okay, you go. Be quick."

"I will run all the way," he joked.

He got up and jogged back towards the toilets. His foe was just on the bridge. James quickly ran up behind him at the highest point, grabbed him.

"Goodbye, pig," he said as he shoved the man off the bridge. There was a heavy thud as the man hit the ground below; blood was pouring from his head! James turned to go quickly back. There was one other person coming—it was Joanna.

"James, what has happened? Did you push that man? You did, didn't you!"

As he reached her, he turned her round to go back.

"James, I realised I needed the toilet and came after you."

He ushered her back to the picnic place and sat to listen again, but there was a commotion behind and that group left hurriedly as something had happened to their friend.

"James, I know you pushed him. Is he hurt badly? I need to know."

"He was drunk and fell. I tried to grab him but missed."

"We should tell the police—he might be dead!"

"I think he is okay; his friends are with him. It is his own fault; it is nothing to do with us—we cannot help."

The day was ruined.

"James, I want to go back to the hotel now. I would rather go straight home but need to collect things from the hotel. James, you frighten me!"

"I did not want to talk to anyone because I might get accused and I cannot prove anything. You saw how nasty they were; they would love to blame me. I don't want to take the chance."

They drove to the hotel and collected their things. She was not going to settle; he agreed to book out and go home. By the time they had driven back to town she was calmer and agreed to stay with him for the day. She was no longer mentioning the incident, but was thinking a lot; she was muddled—she was sure she had seen something she wished she had not!

James was suffering in silence. He eventually took her to her home.

"Bye, Jo. I will call you in the week, okay?"

"Bye, James. Yes, see you here in a day or so. Goodnight."

He drove slowly home, his mind working overtime. He had work to do and proceeded to do it but his mind was elsewhere. He could not care less about the man who had taken the fall, but wished Joanna had not seen it. Had she really seen it or was she guessing? He was not about to ask her; he just needed it to go away. For her, though, it was not going away—who could she talk to? Bob was the obvious choice but he was a policeman! She eventually chose to talk to Bob; after all, he was James's friend. She decided to phone him.

"Bob, it is Joanna. I am sorry to trouble you. I don't want to talk on the phone, but I am worried about James."

"Okay, come anytime to the police station. My office is private. I presume you do not want James to know, so here would be the safest—any day between 5 p.m. and 7 p.m. Ask for me; we won't be interrupted. Is that okay for you?"

"Yes, thank you, Bob. I will be there at 6."

"Okay, Jo, whatever it is we will sort it out— don't worry. See you at 6."

James spent all Monday waiting to see Joanna but worried what she would be like. Had he ruined everything? Had she actually seen nothing—well, nothing incriminating perhaps! Her day went quickly and soon she found herself outside the police station. As she headed to the desk, a voice said:

"Come through, Jo. I was waiting for you."

Inside the office, door closed.

"What can I do for you, Jo?"

"Do you think James could be violent? I saw something quite shocking this weekend when we were away. There was a group of annoying aggressive people behind us ruining the concert and throwing things at us. I thought James either did not see it or he chose to ignore it. But all of a sudden he had to go to the toilet; evidently the worst of the people behind had just gone. James was in a rush; he caught him on the bridge. A few moments before I decided to go as well. I was getting to the bridge when it looked as though James pushed him off and growled something in his ear. I tried to get him to tell me what had happened; he assured me he was innocent and it was nothing to do with him and in fact he tried to stop him falling. We came home; it has messed us up… Who is James? What is he capable of? Or is he innocent?"

"Don't worry, Jo. James has a very strong feeling of right and wrong. If someone hurts him or someone he has feelings for, he harbours the need to put things right or take revenge. I do not think he means to hurt anyone badly; he normally does not have a thought of harm in his head. I have seen little things—when he has been se-verely pushed he eventually reacts. When or why or what sets him off I don't know, but he would never hurt you. He might hurt someone to protect you. He is my friend; I will watch him for his and your sake. Don't give up on him—he has a heart of gold. I am glad you spoke to me, Jo. Get him to arrange another foursome soon. Dianna would like that as well. And by the way, this meeting never happened. I am sure it's all okay but any-time you want, please call."

"Thank you, Bob."

"Nice to see you, Jo, but now I must at least try to catch criminals," he laughed.

She left feeling happier.

It was a strange week for both James and Joanna. He did call on her midweek as usual and they had agreed that it would be a good idea to in-vite Bob and Dianna for Sunday lunch. Saturday was a much quieter day than usual even without mentioning what had or had not happened the weekend before. They were both polite as they were obviously very fond of each other. Both, however, had felt very restricted. Sunday morn-ing they were both happier knowing Bob and Dianna would be there soon. The doorbell rang and James let them in. Bob entered and played the part of the innocent joker perfectly and it pulled the foursome together. The rest of the weekend went as normal; James and Joanna were easing back towards how they had been but they knew that Joanna would probably always have a doubt or worry at the back of her mind even if not showing it.

Bob and Dianna prepared to leave late evening.

"Thanks for having us, you two. Food was great as ever and company first class, but we have to go and prepare for another week of drudgery, called work."

"And I must go too, James," Joanna added. "My students are arriving early. Call on me anytime when you can through the week, James."

The three of them left. James listened to them chatting happily as they walked to their cars. Bob saw Joanna drive off first, then joined Dianna in her car and drove towards town, his arm waving to James out of the window. James closed the door, and with some relief went to bed.

James threw himself into work for most of the week, trying to push the problems with Joanna to the back of his mind. He allowed far less time for music as music brought everything back to him and caused emotions of all types—a bit of a muddle at a time when he needed straight thinking. He did call in on Joanna and both acted oblivious to any problems but both knew the problems were still there.

Joanna had made a suggestion she hoped would be accepted. It was to alter the pattern of the past few weekends—perhaps a fresh start.

"James, I have been thinking. Every weekend

we have put the pressure on you to cook and entertain at your house. Well, how about I cook and entertain you here for a change? I would really like it if you would."

"Sounds good to me, Jo, and it would get me away from work for a day or so. Saturday I will arrive 12, okay?"

"Yes, I will look forward to it."

Saturday, James was out in the barn. One more hour's work and he could go in and change to go to Joanna's. Washed and into his car early enough for the short drive, he pulled into the short drive at the front of her house, immediately seeing her neighbour, an old foe of his, standing looking miserable. James got out of his car and said:

"Good morning, Mr Smith—you are looking well."

"You know my name then? Have we met? I think we have."

"No, I don't, so probably never wanted to!"

"It was you, wasn't it?"

"You think it was me what, Allan?"

"Someone attacked me from behind at night leaving work."

"Why would I attack you? I have no reason. But if you are like this with everyone I expect someone will batter you sooner than later—you ask for it."

"Oh, it was you all right. I know now. My chance will come."

With that he marched into his house, slamming the door. Joanna came out.

"What was all that about, James? He looked even nastier today."

"He thinks I attacked him one night."

"You didn't, did you, James? I know you could."

"No, of course not. He is delusional; he imagines everyone is against him. But now, meeting him, I think he is right—most people would feel like hitting him."

James had now lied to Joanna for the first time and was already regretting it. The confrontation would mean a very quick lunch, again with more thinking than conversation. After lunch they played their duet on her piano; it went some way to getting them back to how they had been before. She then played Chopin to him. He found himself becoming emotional more than usual and very quickly—not surprising under the circumstances for him. The tears ran down his face; he pretended not to notice them. She finished playing.

"That was perfect, Jo, and also reminds me I must get my piano tuned. I see a difference in mine."

He nonchalantly wiped his tears away as though they were just an annoyance of no consequence, but she knew the difference—this was a very emotional man, emotions mostly created by music. Without mentioning it to him she would experiment with different genres of music and watch carefully for different reactions. She managed to introduce a few different types of music and did notice various reactions. Some that she knew he did not like made him irritable. It made her think that under different circumstances perhaps he would be aggressive rather than the very passive man he always seemed to be.

They had a good weekend and parted as very close friends. He left for another busy week's work. As he walked to his car he spotted her neighbour watching him from behind the curtains. James could not resist waving to him but with a derisory look on his face, taunting him. The picture Joanna saw from behind was one of offered friendship. And that was what James wanted her to see or assume.

Unfortunately this was not going to be the end of the problem. Two days later, Allan, Joanna's neighbour, made a point of waiting for her outside the house.

"You do know it was that boyfriend that attacked me the other night, don't you?"

"No, I don't. He would not hurt a fly. Why would he attack you? He tried to be friendly at the weekend."

"No, he did not. He was trying to bait me, making fun of it… Well, we will see who laughs last, Joanna."

"He doesn't know you. Why hurt you? It does not make sense."

"Because I complained about you and your pupils parking. Don't pretend that you were not in on it and not just him."

"Don't be ridiculous. I am going in now—I have pupils waiting. If you have a problem, take it up with James, not me."

"Oh, I will. Just tell him to watch his back—it is not finished."

"Check your facts, you stupid man, or you will end in serious trouble."

With that she went in to her pupils, although she could not stop thinking that James just might have been guilty of beating him on her behalf—after all, she had seen how he could be!

Privately, James was also thinking back through his problems and violent actions. He had taken a lot and started in frightened innocence, but each time there was a problem that he needed to solve he had become more adept and capable. He no longer walked around in fear of any vengeful act against him; not only was he becoming able to choose the best action for whichever problem, but he had grown bigger and much stronger over the last two years. He had got a commanding strut in his demeanour. Underneath he was still the pacifist, anti-violent James he had always been.

"I think I have a split personality," he thought. "Why do I feel so worried about confrontations and only want to get away from friction or arguments when in fact if it erupts I win out easily? One minute I am a pacifist, the next I am seeking physical vengeance as though someone has pressed a button and I have no choice but to change. What is causing the change? The one thing I do know is I am often an emotional tearful wreck and then an emotional aggressive force that needs to be fed and is inescapable."

He was spending a lot of time in self-examination.

"I know which I would always rather be—I hate aggression and people getting hurt. So what makes me do it? Perhaps I need a psychiatrist. I only want to be liked and loved like I love my music. Perhaps I should listen to more music and keep away from people as much as possible. The pub seemed a place to keep away from as it was always full of confrontational people—a lot of them friendly but they all had likes and dislikes that could change to ugly arguments and fights, particularly after a lot of alcohol was consumed…"

Joanna had also done a lot of thinking.

"Okay, what if James had been protecting me? What if he had hit the neighbour for complaining? Perhaps I should make an allowance for it. I doubt if he really wanted to damage the man at the picnic badly—that is, even if he did do it."

She was not really sure. Then she had a man friend that showed that he would do anything to protect her. On the one hand she would need to talk to him seriously about controlling himself; then rather than driving her away she would probably appreciate and even find his strong protectiveness attractive. He had developed most other assets—tall, handsome, loving, plus the ability to earn money. She had been right to worry and question him. He was becoming much more self-assured; in fact, he was pretty well everything a young lady would like in a man.

"James, just stay sensitive," she thought aloud. "I think I am in love with you."

Perhaps only relaxing music this weekend with no one else around—friend or foe. Unfortunately, relaxing music all the time would make him become morose. He was starting to need more rumbustious music and singing to feed his increasing extrovert behaviour. It lifted him like a drug his ambitious nature needed it; without it, he felt he was stagnating. Pavarotti and the other tenors were an antidote to that with the power of their voices. He no longer wanted to be the meek, nice, quiet guy. He enjoyed being the man on his toes, upbeat as much as possible. This coming weekend was going to be different—a more powerful character he was becoming would mean different expectations of both him and Joanna. It could go well; it probably would. They both wanted a fresh start; neither would know until they met!

The third person considering the problems was Bob. He had made inquiries of the man that had fallen, or was he pushed from the bridge in Kenwood Park. The official story so far was that the man had been very drunk and fallen somehow, and there were no witnesses to say one way or the other; therefore, the man died after falling while drunk. Bob was once again having doubts, but for now was giving his friend the benefit of the doubt.

The week, as usual, seemed to be flying by. James had visited Joanna in the middle of the week, and neighbour Allan was behind the curtains watching him come and go. It seemed he was still off work sick; it would be a relief when he started work again, then James could come without feeling watched. While James was there, he had persuaded Joanna to come to his house at the weekend as they always did before. Also, it would be away from the prying eyes of Allan, the nasty neighbour.

Joanna, as arranged, arrived on Saturday morning, and they both had the privacy they needed and relaxed once again. They both hoped normality had returned for good… to all intents and purposes, James seemed just the same—very easily influenced. And if anything, even happier with music. He looked different to her, but inside, evidently, he was just the same quiet, reserved, and thoughtful man he had been when younger—a quiet loner. Apart from Bob and Joanna, he never met with another friend. He knew a lot of people, but none of them did he call a friend.

"Do you not need friends during the week, James? Do you spend every evening alone?"

"Yes, I could go out if I felt like it, but I have no one I want to spend time with. Most people out at night are likely to be troublemakers or argumentative. I never find people with the same likes and dislikes as me, apart from you and Bob. I am happy the way I am. Besides, I always have work that I can do anytime—day or night."

She supposed she was not so very different,

although she did have friends she met for coffee. Most of her time she spent with her pupils. Although happy with James, she still had not got over what happened with the man in the park. She kept finding more reasons to spend time with other friends and less time with James; so far, James was far too busy to notice.

Now, two evenings a week, she met up with a group of friends. Some nights they would play cards or go to the cinema; another evening they would go for a meal. Inevitably, James heard that she was spending time with these friends. He was not surprised or concerned but did worry that Joanna was avoiding him or losing interest, and that did concern James. But he was not about to mention it to her for fear of escalating any problem. He decided to call on Bob for a quiet word to get his feelings on the matter. He drove to the police station; unfortunately, he arrived just in time to see Joanna entering the building, also on her way to talk to Bob. James stopped and parked up to wait to see how long she would be there. Half an hour later, Joanna came out; Bob waved to her as she walked away.

James drove home; he would visit Bob another day. Joanna had not been with Bob long enough for any significant reason; James was sure all would be revealed tomorrow when he would casually visit Bob.

James's mind was not on his work the next day; soon it would be time to see Bob.

"Is Inspector Thomas in his office… Bob Thomas, that is."

"Yes, is he expecting you?"

"No, it's a quick private visit."

"Okay, I will tell him you are here."

"Hi, James. What can I do for you? Come through to the office."

They walked into the office without speaking. Once inside, James spoke first.

"I feel Joanna is cooling on me. Last night I came to see you but saw her here to see you. Is there a problem?"

"No, I don't think so. She is worried about you and rather like you wanted to talk about it. She thinks you have changed a lot over the last few weeks. She has started meeting with her girlfriends more to take the pressure off your relationship, which is working, but still does not answer why you have seemed to change. If you ask me—as I am sure you will, as that is what you came here for—then I think you both need interests outside one another."

"Yes, I suppose so, as long as she has not cooled totally. Anything is worth a try. I would not want to be without her."

"I know, and she feels exactly the same, James. So go with the flow. I am sure all is well for you both of you."

"Well, Bob, that is roughly what I needed to hear! If you see her, no need to mention I had been worried or that we had discussed it, okay?"

"Understood, James. And as I said, no problem—just go with the flow and enjoy."

"Yes, a few different interests will be good."

Although still no major problem between them, they were both aware of drifting apart. Both wanted a change; they were finding reasons not to meet so often. Joanna was meeting up with friends several times a week. This had come to the attention of James, which had led him to drive into and around town most evenings. He had got to recognise her friends, some of which she met much more than others, mostly females of roughly her age, occasionally a male friend or two. Whether it was by accident or design, he could not tell—only ever seeing them in a café or bar, that she always left to walk home alone. This time, James waited a few more minutes before driving back home, where he would sit and listen to music. His mood and emotions changing all the time. The more he thought about Joanna, the more emotional he got. His relationship with her seemed to be slowly dividing; what could he do to re-establish it?

Most weeks, he would see Joanna going to Bob's office… why?? He could not ask. And neither would explain. Therefore, it was left to James and his active imagination. Listening to the music he liked made him feel worse; he was fast feeling more and more depressed when they met at weekends he found it difficult to give the impression of being totally happy, and that made her feel different and not so happy with him. She had similar thoughts to him.

"What can be done? Anything?" She was feeling increasingly unwanted. Doubts were increasing all around… a break at least would be helpful, but they both saw that a break would be the beginning of the end—a point of no return—as James was thinking, there must be someone else in Joanna's life!!!

A serious talk between them was becoming very necessary, but neither felt they could start without possibly upsetting the other, so they never did. Instead, it left them both with stressed imaginations, with James watching her, which was the worst thing he could do. It was not long before both Joanna and her friends had seen James in strange situations, obviously spying on her.

On her weekend visit, she brought the subject up as carefully as she could, but it developed into an argument that was in itself a new situation for them. After the preliminary verbal sparring, it became quite serious.

"I even see you visiting Bob. In fact, I think you spend more time with him than me."

"Bob is a good friend, and I need someone to talk to! Don't you trust me? Don't you trust Bob? He is your friend more than mine, and he thinks the world of Dianna."

"I do trust you both, but why can't you talk to me like you talk to him?"

"Because, James, I never know how you will react. And what sort of man watches his girlfriend secretively… an innocent lady like me, it's not healthy! My friends have seen you and are beginning to make remarks!"

"I only watch because I don't want to ask or upset you."

"You don't need to watch. Talk to me like a normal man, for goodness' sake."

Then a long silence followed. The weekend would soon be over and nothing had been solved. Music had been played but that had only made them both emotional to the point of turning it off.

"James, I will have to go soon. I don't want to leave you here like this. I am just as fond of you as I ever was. Let us go back to how we were, please, and no more watching, alright?"

"Okay, I will call in during the week to see you at one lunchtime, if that's alright."

"Of course it is."

They kissed more politely than lovingly and certainly not passionately. With a smile, she left.

"Thanks for dinner, James. As good as ever. Bye! Love you!"

"Love you too, Jo. Bye."

They had both used the word love, but without much conviction—just the expected word, the word that stuck in James's mind was "fond," as in "I am fond of you, James," that seemed a massive step down even though just a word. James was an analyser of everything, including words, and this one did not help him get to sleep.

He was up early as usual doing his jobs in the barn, then spent the rest of the day resting. The temptation of driving into town, of course, in his mind—not to watch but to drive through in case he might see something of interest! He should have heeded his mother's words: "Be careful what you look for, because look and you will see! Don't look and there will be nothing to find." All very similar to "don't paint the devil on the wall lest he should appear." James found these easy to ignore or understand and all according to what state of mind he was in or how emotional he felt! Self-doubts led to dark thoughts, and these thoughts were taking James over. His inner self-destruct button was being pressed every day of this week. So far, he had driven to town for no necessary reason. Each time he had gained a fact that had provided dark thoughts, even though completely unfounded. His mind refused to dismiss them; in fact, in the evenings while listening to music, all thoughts increased and grew out of proportion. The music was making him feel more vulnerable. It was now exactly midweek and he could not put off the promised visit to Joanna any longer without arousing suspicion.

He changed his clothes and smartened himself up more than usual. He drove slowly and nervously to town. Her neighbour this time was not hiding behind his curtains. James thought he must be back at work. He neared Joanna's and could hear a pupil playing the piano and her voice quietly giving advice. James waited at the door for a while without knocking in the hope that the lesson would end before he disturbed them. The piano stopped and James rang the bell. A moment later came to the door. As it opened, James immediately recognised the man with her; he was often with her and friends in the café.

"That's a coincidence," he thought… a coincidence James did not like. The man left.

"Bye, Joanna. Thank you, that was a great

lesson today," he said over his shoulder, knowing those few words would have a detrimental effect on James and his meeting with Joanna. It could have been meant as harmless but no—not in James's mind. THIS MAN WAS A SMART ASS!

James stayed quite a while but it was tense between them. James knew who was to blame—this pupil, whatever his name was.

Later that evening, James was driving innocently through town past the café meeting place Joanna had established. He was looking and what did he see? Oh yes, he saw what he expected to see. Joanna with her friends, and one of them was the pupil from earlier. James drove round the corner out of sight then walked partway back. As he did, he saw Joanna step out of the café to make a phone call—a quite long one. In fact, she was phoning Bob with more worries about James. It ended with Bob telling her he would call on James the next day to see how he was and what state of mind he was in.

James drove home even more stressed than before. He might not have got the truth of everything, but he was sure he had. He was full of ideas and spent the night awake. When Bob arrived in the morning, he was not at his brightest. Bob, though, was as bright as always; he acted as though he had no reason to think there was a problem between James and Joanna—he was used to this from his job.

"Hey, James, how are you doing? We have not spoken lately. I came past the barn just now. I see you are still getting plenty of work. Have you been out there yet this morning? Do you need a hand for a while?"

"No, I have not been out yet. Have you time to help move things around a bit? It's a bit clogged up at the moment."

"Okay, let us have coffee then. I can give you an hour lifting."

"Well, coffee is ready so it's a deal."

"How are you and Joanna now? All good, I hope."

"Not really, Bob—worse if anything. She came at the weekend but it was a bit strange. And I saw her yesterday but I think she has moved on. She meets the same people all the time, one of them—a man—a pupil that seems to be involved."

"I can't believe that, James. Dianna sees her quite often and I am sure she would know if there was anyone on the scene. Anyway, she is not that sort of a girl, and why would she still be coming to stay with you? There's not a cat's chance in hell that she is at all interested in anyone else. She is an attractive girl; plenty of men would find her attractive, and they from time to time try to attract her, but that is their problem, not hers! She would not even notice them."

"You know as well as I do—stop looking for problems. There are none. If you are not careful, you will create some! I think we have moved everything from outside, Jimbo. Do you want a hand putting a batch into the tank before I go?"

"No, it's alright. I can manage—I have the pulley, and you need to go chasing criminals before they get away, Bob."

"Yes, I had better get chasing some or the chief will be chasing me... Oh, James, give Joanna some space and trust. She deserves it."

"Okay, Bob. You know best. Thanks for calling."

"No problem, Jim."

As soon as Bob was in his car, he was on the phone to Joanna.

"Hi, Jo. I saw James this morning—he is okay. He just worries a lot about you. I told him you needed space but were alright. I must get to work now."

"Thanks, Bob. Space would be great if I get it. He will probably take your word for it. See you soon, and thanks again."

James stayed away from town for a couple of days. The only problem was when he went in on the third evening he saw Joanna with the pupil in the café. He was angry, even though there were a couple of her girlfriends in there at the same time. Once again, his midweek visit to her was spoiled as this pupil, Mike, was there again for his lesson, grinning like a Cheshire cat or rather as James saw it… like the cat that got the cream. Either way, it made James's blood boil. He tried not to let Joanna see his annoyance, but she could tell something was wrong and realised it was Mike causing it, making matters worse by deliberately upsetting James.

"Hi, James. When are you going to have a lesson… what has brought you here today?" Mike said with a laugh…

James said nothing but thought to himself: "Mike, you will regret every stupid remark soon… sooner than you think."

Joanna was pleased and relieved to see James did not react and chose to ignore Mike. Unfortunately, James chose the third path—he made polite excuses and drove back to work. That evening, James messaged Joanna.

"Will I see you this weekend as usual?"

She messaged back.

"Perhaps we should try something differ- ent this week—why not come and join me and my friends at the café, then go to the cinema or something else to break the mould for a while. Since the problem in the park seems to have made everything too intense, you choose, James, and I will be happy to do it whatever."

"Okay, I will message you tomorrow."

He had plenty of work to take his mind off things. And he had already decided to play music again despite how morose it often made him feel. At the moment, he could only face the slow, quiet solo pieces, or at the most, quartets. Anything more irritated his mind to the point of anger. He knew how important it was to show no anger, particularly none in front of Joanna.

"Hi, Joanna. Okay, let us meet in your café with your friends for a while, then go to a film with or without them, then a Chinese meal. Does that sound okay to you?"

"Sure, James. It will be a welcome change."

He would have liked to ask which of her friends would be there, but thought it better to say nothing and show no one else mattered other than her. He did not want to go with preconceived ideas about Mike, or what he intended to do to teach him a lesson in case it showed—having painted the devil on the wall—his devil might appear and do something bad!!!

All Saturday morning, James spent imagining everything that might go wrong. He coupled that with his dislike of what he had agreed to—none of it suited him. Why had he been willing to comply with her suggestions? As far as he was concerned, he was sure the whole day was bound to be a disaster. James and Joanna had become opposites, whereas for the first few months they had seemed perfectly suited! Right now, James wished he could phone her to say they ought to finish the relationship and move forward separately… the devil had been on the wall—it was over, he was sad but at the same time angry. Although now full of trepidation, he drove to the café to fulfil what he had agreed to, even knowing how alien it was to him.

As soon as he had opened the café door, the raucous Duke Box music hit him—it offended his hearing. He said nothing but wished he had not come. Even the welcomes and introductions were stilted. The conversation with Joanna was odd—whether because of him or her, he could not tell—but the day was getting rapidly worse. As soon as he could, he took Joanna to one side to make his apologies.

"This is not me at all. I owe it to you to leave you here with them and get on with our lives separately. Sorry, Joanna, I should have known before. None of these people would I want to spend an hour with, let alone a day. I have a lot to do at home, and that Duke Box is grating on my nerves. Perhaps we can talk sometime. Now enjoy your day and friends."

As he turned to leave and reached the door, Mike called out.

"Are you off then? That didn't take long, did it? The usual anti-social git. How does Joanna put up with it?"

"You have never been any good for her. Good riddance, I say."

James turned and walked purposely back to him and put his face right up to Mike's and whispered through his teeth, "One more word and I will stop your mouth working altogether."

Mike looked shocked.

"Anything to say, mouthy Mike?"

"No, I thought not."

James walked back to the door and said, "Goodbye."

She had heard nothing else other than the loud Duke Box, not a word was spoken.

"Well, that is that," he thought—no lady friend now.

He was soon back at work. He would not visit town again unless really necessary. It would be a lonely life again for him. He sorted through his music for things easy to listen to; his mood was different, some things he could not take at the moment, even some of the things he had really liked before.

Whereas his mood could drastically change, then also music could completely change him. For the next few days, he would only want to play middle-of-the-road classical. That did not stir him too much one way or the other, but he could close his eyes and relax.

Five days went by and then Bob turned up.

"Hi, Jim. I saw Joanna yesterday. She said you had split up—surely not!"

"Yes, we have. I won't bore you with the details, but it is for the best; we are not right for each other."

"When did you decide that?"

"Saturday in the café, with her friends. They were not for me, and she is happy with them. I tried my best to blend in with them but it was hopeless. Anyway, she agreed! So that is that."

"Are you sure that is what she wanted?"

"Look, Bob, she did not want to spend the weekend with me and wanted a change. Instead, she expected me to join in with her friends, including sly Mike, to spend time in the café with a poxy Duke Box!!! Then go with them all for the evening—she might like that. But it's not for me, and if I stayed around Sly Mike much longer I would probably kick his arse, that is what he continually asks for. And if she wants him, she can have him!"

"I very much doubt she wants him or anyone else, James."

"Well, she should say so or make it obvious. She seems happy enough with him chasing her."

"Are you staying for coffee, Bob?"

"If you are having one."

"Well, I am about to have a break, so let's have one… Are you listening to too much music at the moment? I am a bit, but I have got more choosy. It's about like alcohol or cannabis—if I am in a bad mood, everything makes me worse, and if I am in a good mood, it makes me even better! The problem is, at the moment I am nearly always in a bad mood, so you can imagine how I end up feeling then!"

"Well, Jim, put something light on. I don't want a fight or argument," he laughed, not realizing how serious it could be.

James might well have felt calm and not too upset at the loss of Joanna, but without realizing it he was more anguished than he knew… someone was to blame!!! And someone would pay dearly if James caught them at the wrong time or him in the wrong mood and listening to the type of music that fed him with aggressive confidence to push him over the edge, needing to exercise his violent streak.

They quietly drank their coffee while listening to Chopin, all very relaxed. Bob was thinking, "James is such an easy-going character—why on earth doesn't he get on with Joanna? They were so close for a long time, perhaps it is her that is the problem, but then that seems equally odd." James had not said much, but Bob was sure James blamed Joanna for the breakup.

"I had better get back to work, James. Are you going to ring Joanna sometime?"

"No point—she has her friends and they are nothing like me. It was her choice; if she wants anything, she knows she can call."

"Bye for now, James. I will call in at the end of the week."

"Okay, see you, Bob."

As much as he did not want to drive to town, he needed some shopping and would have to go. He would, though, leave it as late as possible rather than bump into anyone. The supermarket was open until midnight, so plenty of time. 11 o'clock, he decided to go. As he suspected, the car park was empty; it was a good time for him to go shopping. He had been listening to a disc passing the time before finally switching it off. It felt strange without—it felt like he had company, he felt better about himself. The louder, the better. He strutted to the shop doorway, feeling up for anything. He had all the answers. As he got to the door, he saw the problem that needed to be fixed—sly Mike was leaving the shop. James stepped back into the shadows and waited for him. James quickly formed a plan. He moved back to his car and opened the boot. He bent over it facing the other way so as not to be seen and recognised as Mike. Mike went to pass him. James stood up, turned to meet him.

"Hello, smart ass. Fancy seeing you here. I just thought I would give you what I promised."

"Oh yes, and what is that?"

Without reply, James punched him hard on the side of his jaw. He was glad, as usual, put his gloves on. He felt the side of Mike's face collapse as he broke his jaw. Having put his gloves on meant his knuckles would not be as damaged, if at all. His boot was already open; as Mike fell, James tipped him in and closed the boot before anyone could see what was happening. He did not bother with any shopping; instead, he drove straight home to the barn, music still playing as he stopped outside. He let it finish before he switched the car off. He dropped the unconscious Mike by the tank, hooked him by his collar, winched him up and lowered him into the caustic tank, then lowered the iron frame full of doors on top of him. The weight of all this squashed his body down into the ever-thickening layers of stripped paint sludge. He heard some gurgling noises but paid no attention to them. He mixed another bag of caustic pearls and tipped it into the tank. That would make sure it was strong enough to eat away anything in the tank. The last job to do today was now to clean the car boot out and put junk back in again.

"That's a good old job done, Jimmy boy."

He was soon indoors and ready for bed. He was eager to sleep and did not bother to look at his phone or put the TV on. He slept soundly until his usual breakfast time at 8 o'clock. Coffee was all he wanted. The latest batch of doors would be ready to wash off; he winched them out, also watching to make sure nothing like Mike, for instance, drifted up when the pressure was off. But as James had thought, the body would be stuck fast in the sludge, never to move again. Even if it did, then the iron frame loaded continually on top would fix it again day and night. Then, of course, most would soon be eaten away by the acids!

James was fortunate, or was it ice cold? Whichever, within an hour of dropping Mike in the tank! He hardly thought of it again, even working with the tank—it was as though it had never happened. He did sometimes think of Joanna, perhaps things would be different if she contacted him, but if she left it up to him to make a move, then more than likely he would do nothing. He did miss her, but under these circumstances, he could see no point in trying something and then forgetting it; nothing mends the same. There are too many other things to worry about than trying to change someone's mind. He accepted it all at its worst. Most nights since they parted, he had cried himself to sleep on a tear-drenched pillow. He had blamed the emotional music he always played lately, which was true, but it was Joanna's innocent face he was seeing.

He practiced the piano on his own!! His work earned him plenty of cash. "What else do I need?" he answered himself. "NOTHING."

Later that week, Bob came. "How are you getting on, Jim? I saw Joanna yesterday, and she said it was you that ended it between you and that you must have frightened Mike off as he has not been for his lesson, and she has heard nothing of him all week. He hasn't even been to the café. You have not seen him anywhere, have you?"

"No, I haven't been to town since I saw Joanna. I suppose I will have to sometime; I need some food shopping… Does he live in town?"

"I think he lives on the main road south, fairly near the town centre."

"Does he live on his own?"

"I think so, well at least Jo thinks so."

"No one has reported him missing though, have they?"

"Not yet, but you never know. I hope you have not moved him on, James. I know how much you disliked him; he was evidently always chasing Joanna. But she could not stand him, she is pleased he stopped coming, she thought he was trouble."

Bob left for work. James soon finished his and was trying to think of something to do in the afternoon. He had a lot more time on his hands since he was no longer seeing Joanna; he was in fact spending more and more time bored and alone. He still played most genres of music but was more careful not to play much emotional, thought-arousing pieces or emotional songs. For now, he preferred the boisterous classics. It suited his current frame of mind. *Vangelis* often got played but created an emotional state almost totally upsetting. He hoped this problem would soon pass and he would be back to his pre-Joanna eclectic choices. The problem at the moment was he constantly thought of her.

This afternoon, he would spend an hour or more practicing the piano, trying to copy some of his favourites. He started well with it but became emotional; more to the point, he had to stop—unable to see for tears, unable to concentrate. No doubt if he had been more professional, he would have been able to play through floods. At this stage, it took little to put him off, rendering him useless. He was, of course, trying to find someone or something to blame for his problems. Mike was right—perhaps he was antisocial. After all, who did he like? Only Bob, Joanna, and Dianna. He could think of no one else. Did Bob even know how few people James liked?

"I doubt it," he thought… "What do I want out of life? I thought I knew."

He was walking round the house in a daze, trying to understand himself and decide what would make him happy. He had already taken a wrong path—in fact, a path of no return. Other than Bob, who called in most weeks, the only people James ever saw were a few customers, and none of those were ever very talkative. It was a lonely life, and he was not playing as much music as before in fear of being upset. Most had a depressing effect on him, making him reflect back over the violent incidents he had been involved in. He was at a loss sometimes to think or remember what exactly had caused them; he was spending time daily regretting his actions. The shocked faces of those he had hurt or killed were imprinted on his mind—they had not been a problem before, but now they were.

Spending so much of his time alone was not helping his state of mind. It was causing introspective thinking and self-examination. That could be okay, but this much was damaging.

He was becoming more irrational; he was missing Joanna but felt she was better off without him. He was seeing his own life in an impossible situation; it was also affecting his friendship with Bob, his faithful friend. Bob, in turn, was noticing James becoming more detached. Bob was putting it down to the breakup with Joanna and depression, even though he did not realise it was worse. When Bob did call, they had coffee as usual and played music; other than that, there was hardly ever any conversation. Bob had on a couple of occasions spoken to Joanna about it. She was concerned and had never moved on; James was still on her mind. She never ever made any approach to him, as she had been led to believe that he did not want her around. She was also beginning to see he was different to what he had been—the signs were that he was suffering, trying to compensate for the life he seemed to have lost. It was like starting again. Without knowing what he really wanted and, more to the point, what could he now achieve, to him everything had been a one-time chance. The chance of love and a partner—"ruined." What was left was a business and a very lonely life. Even that was on a knife edge; he could be found out at any time. One or another of his murderous actions could come to life and ruin any chance of normality in future. He knew he had done these things; he somehow absolved himself from blame. He could justify anything. He was beginning to see himself as a judge and jury, and somehow he had been forced into action, like some sort of drug. The one thing he had become sure of was music made him very emotional and did have an effect on him—good and bad. Perhaps sometime he would try an experiment: a test to see how different music could make him be—just how psychologically different did different types of music make him. Placid to physical to extreme aggression. Perhaps he was trying to find excuses for his past behaviour and, of course, temper.

He had a lot of work to do, so decided to let the next day or two play out—hoping for a quiet time. If things changed, then he would change accordingly. He thought he was in control, but was he? He worked hard that day, giving little thought to anything else. The day went; he was not hungry but went through the motions of eating tea. While listening to *Einaudi*, the piano music he loved. Unfortunately, it reminded him of the love of his life, Joanna—it was also her favourite. He now was feeling lost and emotional; he decided he would have to go out, even to drive for a while.

In the past, he often found himself driving towards town and Joanna, then forcing himself to drive in the opposite direction as soon as he realised. All this chopping and changing and playing different music was muddling his demeanour, creating an even more depressed James. He needed to be an orderly person without sudden changes. Now, of course, he badly wanted to vent his anger and frustration on someone or something; the longer he thought, the worse it got. He sat in the car aimlessly, listening to whatever music was playing, not realising how much worse it was making him feel. He watched everyone critically as their annoying lives played themselves out in front of him—so many of these people, in his eyes, deserved a kick in the arse or at least a slap for the fuss they were making for no good reason.

"'I need to drive away,' he thought, 'before I lose it and do something I and they would regret.' He drove away thinking, 'Let them stew in their own juice,' as he drove out of the car park. A couple walked straight across in front of his car; he tooted, but instead of getting out of the way, the man decided to stop and made matters worse by banging his fist on the bonnet of the car, then stood menacingly in front. The girl, at least, had the sense to keep moving to be clear of any possible collision. The man, however, was intent on taking his time. After looking around, James also felt he should take his time—too many people around for him to do a proper job.

James said nothing but looked the man in the eyes and thought to himself, "If he does not know what to expect, now he soon will." The man moved and stood sneering as James drove out and round the corner, where he stopped, put on his gloves and got out. He walked back fifty metres; he rather wanted to meet the man walking well away from his car. As predicted, he met the couple without a problem. He hit the man hard. "That's for the bonnet." The man lay out cold. James knelt down over him and hit him again hard, this time saying, "And that's for the sneer." The girl just stood there, her eyes transfixed on the boyfriend. James knew from experience that a girl at a time like this would not see or recognise anyone. Her shocked eyes were only for the comatose boyfriend. James walked slowly back round the corner to his car, drove unnoticed from the scene, and home. For some reason, he now felt better than he did when he earlier left home.

Perhaps any involvement in life made him feel good. Once home and indoors, he felt happy and relaxed again. Any music he played now was welcome.

A few days later, in the centre of town, he was sat people-watching. The later the evening got, the more homeless appeared, especially younger ones. Also, the later it got, the more foreign, scruffy men came. At first, it looked as though they came offering help. It soon became obvious they were preying on the very vulnerable children and youngsters.

James watched and became agitated at the mistakes these youngsters were making and the bad options they were given. That night, he drove home questioning himself, "Why did I do nothing? What could I have done... Was he sure all he saw was wrong?" Too many questions were muddling his brain—just what should he think... had he let some youngsters down? That night, he slept very little. By morning, he had decided to at least watch again, then make a decision. He had a full day's work to do first. He would then go to town for his night's vigil...

He parked near the town centre as the day and daylight started to recede. There were the usual groups of youngsters, possibly runaways, hanging around—some smoking, goodness knows what, some carrying large bottles of water, most of them acting as though they were carrying something far stronger than water. But then the grubby little bits of cigarettes and smoke-filled bottles could be the problem—they were far too young and poor to be able to afford anything to do with needles unless being lured with gifts by older people on the make, by getting these kids in debt. Glue, perhaps, being their original sin. James had seen glue containers thrown behind bushes in the park. Now he had seen enough; he felt sick. What a waste of youngsters—deliberately misleading them for personal gain… INHUMAN!…

James sat on a bench and tried to chat casually with any of these vulnerable kids. But to do so was difficult without appearing to be another man out for his own evil gains. Without reason, he was starting to feel as bad as the others. He started to sound false. The children were used to all this and became defensive and accusative.

"'What do you want, mister? Do you think we are stupid, you dirty old man? It will cost you!'"

He would let that go—no point in arguing. Anyway, for their own good, they needed to see most people in this light: the light of molesters and users.

James did ask a few questions about the adults hanging around in the evening and got some shocking answers. Some refused to talk in fear more than anything, but the look in their eyes was enough for James to make his decisions. He had narrowed his targets for today to three who looked part of a small gang. Ideal for James, with the element of surprise—they would never know what hit them!!

As it happened, he had attracted the attention of the same group. They in turn were questioning him.

"'Who was he? Where was he from?'"

He tried to present himself as a lonely by-stander, not interested in anything! He guessed they would not believe it and were being menac-ing, feeling their way. They probably saw him as someone working alone, trying to take some of their business from them—well, they would not want that! Soon, they would make a move, and that would be his time to strike back harder than they would expect.

On his way to the centre, he had left his car round one corner up a narrow lane. Besides put-ting his gloves on as usual, he had left his pas-senger door window open and a baseball bat ly-ing on the seat within easy reach. Now back in the centre, he had managed to annoy the chosen group, and they in turn had made remarks about him wearing gloves. It was time he went home out of their way. He had somehow managed to convey a sense of fear and still made some insulting remarks to them. They walked towards him; he lured them on and went round the corner. They were now under the impression they were on a winner. Anyway, there were three of them; they were happy to let him round the corner as they would all be out of sight when they needed to perform their bullying.

Once James rounded the corner, he began to trot up the lane. The chase was on. With chasers jeering behind, slowly catching, it was the pace James had allowed. He reached his car five metres ahead, reached in, took the bat, and immediately swung it hard at the first head that was right behind him. There was a sickening thud—the man dropped like a stone. The second man was still in shock as James hit him with the same power that put him to sleep with his friend. The third turned to make his getaway. James was chasing hard; four strides later, he bashed him on the back of his head. James dragged him back to the other two, kicked their legs apart, and gave them all one more mighty bash to their crutches. That would be a long-lasting memory as to why it had happened and what people like James thought of child users—paedophiles, more than likely. Well, he had given the police or anyone interested a big clue as to what had happened here and why—it should act as a deterrent for a while anyway and slow down an understanding police inquiry. Time to go home now. He parked by the barn and tossed the bat into the tank; it would float but be well cleaned. He entered the house, knowing he was too full of nervous energy to sleep. He would be on a high for days. He put on Rachmaninoff's *Second Piano Concerto* and sat in his armchair with a mug of tea, still hoping later he would be able to get to bed for some sleep. As it was, several hours later, he fell asleep in his chair, music still playing. He woke to the sound of his doorbell.

"'Bloody hell, I bet that's Bob. Surely he is not on my case already.'"

"Good morning, Bob."

"Hi, James."

"Coffee, Bob."

"That would be nice, James. Yes, please."

James went to get it.

"Big night, James? I see you have still got your going-out clothes on," Bob remarked, not going to come straight to the point.

"Going anywhere special?"

"No, I got ready to go out and then changed my mind to stay here. I had had a very tiring day."

"Someone had a very tiring night in town last

night too, James… three sleaze balls. Had a battering up the alley off the square. I am not saying that they did not deserve it. But law and order is my job, so I have to chase it up… This coffee is good today, James."

"Same as usual, Bob."

"I know. I was changing the subject for a minute."

"Why?"

"Well, the batterings had your name written all over them. The three battered were left with balls like footballs… making a very obvious example of them… It looked like James Justice to me!! You always need to act. God, James, more than anyone else I know!!! Say nothing, James, but for God's sake, don't let it always be you. I cannot keep taking a blind eye, whether I like you or not. Now, JAMES, take in what I said. Say nothing and fetch some biscuits… If I can work it out, it was you, then others will sooner or later… Not too many biscuits, that could be seen as bribery… I have a lot of pretending to search for clues to do today all around town."

"Thanks for the biscuits and coffee, James. I had better get back to work. And James, think on—neither you nor anyone else can sort out the evil little mobs controlling the youngsters and vulnerable. Watch out. Most are small but all working for the big boys, and they are danger-ous. We will get them in the end. At the moment, we get one and two more arrive, and worse!! So think on, okay."

Bob left. He understood James and liked him a lot. He knew that among all the extreme actions James was capable of, there was an overriding feeling of justice and well-meaning. His thoughts being… "If I don't do something, then who will?"

For the next two weeks, James would do nothing but watch, follow, and make notes. He was on an unstoppable trail; he would slowly work out where to hurt these mobs the most while listening to his music alone in his room that made him feel stronger and convinced, as well as ex-tremely emotional.

He soon came up with some names and ad-dresses, hopefully real and traceable. No hurry—if a job is worth doing, it has got to be done right!

After two weeks, he had spoken to a few children who, strangely enough, were no longer around. It was too much to hope they were back home with their families, as he hoped. He was now fast reaching the point of payback and ret-ribution from JAMES JUSTICE… HE LIKED THE SOUND OF THAT…

He spent his evenings more and more in tor-ment. Every piece of music he played was stirring him into a stronger emotional state. Perhaps it was the mood he was in that controlled the choice of music and inevitably created the monster in him that surfaced when needed. Now, of course, this monster had found a deserving purpose. And James had grown into a confident physical man. He had experimented with his favourite pieces of music, most of which created almost the same intense emotions, all blended into the same drug-like power.

He drove one more time into town. This time, he did not stop in the centre but visited the supposed secret houses and worked out which ones were most important and which were visited most often. Now clear in his mind which ones he would visit first when the time came, he would go home once all research was completed. Now he was ready and could settle down to the inspirational music he loved. Again, without intention, he was loading up what he was sure would be part of his final act. There was not a chance of overloading. He was used to natural extreme music that made emotions. He started with Einaudi, followed by Demos Russo's "Goodbye My Love, Goodbye," *Jenkins Benedictus*, and the last before leaving the house was Debussy's *Clair de Lune*. Then sat in his car on his way, he played Vangelis' *Capture of Paradise* on a loop and the vision of the fighting *Temeraire*, the famous British warship. James was now on his mission. It was dark, midnight approaching. He slid his car into the predetermined place and parked.

He might appear to be walking slowly in a casual fashion towards the target house, but that was deceiving. He was feeling and flexing his muscles beneath his clothes. He could feel every muscle he had got. Once again, he left the door window open, but this time no bat—instead, on the seat was his sawn-off 12 bore shotgun for last-minute use.

He approached the door and rang the bell, facing away from the spy hole.

"Who is it?" a voice barked.

"John," he replied in a confident voice. James, now standing too close to the spy hole, "Okay." The door opened. "The usual, please. Young and frisky."

"That's easy," the other man chuckled. "Cash. How much is it, dearer now?"

"Afraid so—£500."

"Okay." James put his hand in his pocket, pulled it out with brass knuckles on his fist. No money! He spared the man nothing. The first blow drew a lot of blood; he fell to the floor. James hit him again, men started to appear from the other doors, shocked but joining the fight in defence of their business. James hit as many as possible as fast as possible. The ones on the floor were now being stamped on. James could tell already this was going to be a losing battle. But he knew what he wanted to achieve, and that was still on the cards. For now though, as much damage as possible, and that he was achieving. He was already cut badly. The knives were out and in use. Time to go, James decided. He opened the door and ran out, leaving all inside shocked, needing guidance. "He won't get far, call the boss now. If we chase, it will draw attention." James had not gone far, just back to his car where he sat watching and waiting for part two of his attack. All in the house believing it was all over for now anyway. They licked their wounds and waited for their boss to arrive with a bit of leadership. He soon came. James had now casually walked in a roundabout way back to meet the boss on the doorstep. The boss stood there like a huge ugly pig of a man, James believed he was. "Time to say goodbye, slime ball." James shot him where he stood in the head with the twelve bore, and another with the other barrel. He stuck two more cartridges in and shot through the door. No one wanted to come out or even tried. "Like shooting fish in a barrel." He had heard the saying; now he knew how it felt. Nothing else to do now, the second shock of the night accomplished. They were now clueless—they never expected the first barrage and certainly did not expect the second. Their main man dead and possibly one or two more... no point of return for James, but he expected nothing else... a job well done... he thought. Nothing to gain by staying, so he left. Once back in his house, he phoned his pal Bob, who was not too pleased with what James had done. This time, James hid nothing from him and insisted the police hurry to the target house, no hurry to get here, Bob. "I won't be going anywhere, I will wait for you. Just clear up the target house thoroughly for evidence and youngsters."

"James, you bloody fool, why, why, why!!!"

"Okay, James, of course I trust you... wait for me... you do know what I have to do, don't you? I can't ignore it this time, but for your sake, I do not want you to be arrested, even by me. Prison would be horrendous for everyone. Think something out, please, James!"

James, as usual, had thought everything out. He was settled in his mind as he had been for weeks. James did, however, remember one thing: he went to the barn and emptied all the spare bags of caustic pearls into the tank. "That should finish the body off, particularly if no one checks it for some time." Now satisfied, he went indoors to treat himself to nonstop music; that was all he needed now.

Bob was amazed at the carnage he saw in town. His mind was on only one thing! "What shall I do… what can I do?" Everything was sorted out there with a lot of mumblings in the police ranks. "These bastards have been asking for something like this for a long time. I feel nothing for any of them. They searched the rooms they should have searched before. But, of course, they only found a few youngsters, as most had been passed on and sold to other towns as soon as possible, leaving fewer clues to be found. There was enough here to lock up the remains of this gang for years, perhaps not long enough, but this time something important had been achieved."

Bob spent the night thinking and scratching his head. He kept putting off his visit to James, but the time came when it could no longer be delayed… He rang the doorbell. James let him in; the music was still playing in the background, giving James something to think about.

"James, you are bleeding badly. What do you need?"

"Nothing, Bob. It was inevitable—they soon had their knives out. There were no queens bury rules there."

"Bob, no one had a better friend than you!

Thanks for everything, pal. Sorry for all the trouble I caused. I promise there will be no more. I do, however, have a favour to ask of you. First, we will have coffee one last time, then leave me for an hour before you come back officially. I will then have had my *Einaudi* Treat, of all the wonderful music I have loved. For me, he has been the king of them all. And that is the one thing I want to hear."

They drank their coffee. The last few dregs seemed to take an age but could be delayed no longer. Cups empty, the two men smiled at one another and shook hands—they had to let go. Bob walked bravely out of the door and to his car. He glanced at his watch… he would be back at ten o'clock.

His next thoughts were of Joanna. Once again, his thoughts were, "What do I do about her? How do I explain…" Also, the timing would be important. He decided to leave talking to her until nine forty-five, then go straight to James.

As it happened, they arrived at James's house at the same time. Bob had not explained everything to Joanna, but she had guessed. Bob left her at the door and went in alone. Ten minutes later, he came out. She asked of him, "Is it over, Bob?"

"Yes, Jo, it's over." He had switched the music off. He had left a message for her. Bob passed it to her. She read it to herself and cried uncontrollably. It was a simple note that read, "I love you, Jo. Move on, sweetheart. Please live, listen, and enjoy as you always have. Play our tune with a smile. My will is with the solicitors. Everything is yours. Please accept it and do as you like." James had taken his pills, as he knew he would have to. He could never be imprisoned; no one would understand. He had said goodbye in the only way possible, as he wanted and knew would be best for everyone… Only the ones that mattered knew the truth. By now, Dianna had arrived and was taking Joanna home with her. She turned to say goodbye to Bob.

"Bob, you are crying."

He acted dismissive but was hurting a lot.

"Yes, okay… the music did it!!!

THE END